THE ADVENTURES OF
JONNIE ROCKET

THE
RIDE OF TERROR

The Ride of Terror

Author and creator John Chapman

Illustrations by The Comic Stripper Studio

A CIP catalogue record of this book is available from the British Library

ISBN: 978-0-9573035-2-2

Published by Jonnie Rocket Ltd. 2011

Printed by DCW Penrose & Co. Ltd. Staines, Middlesex

First edition: 2011
Second edition: 2013

www.jonnierocket.com

Meet the Cast!

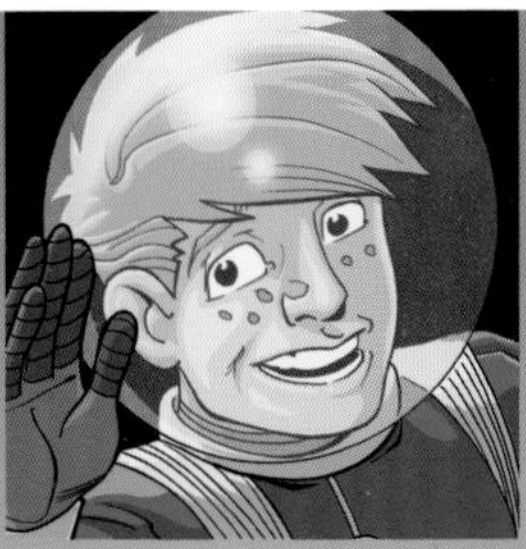

Jonnie Rocket,
Galactic
Adventurer

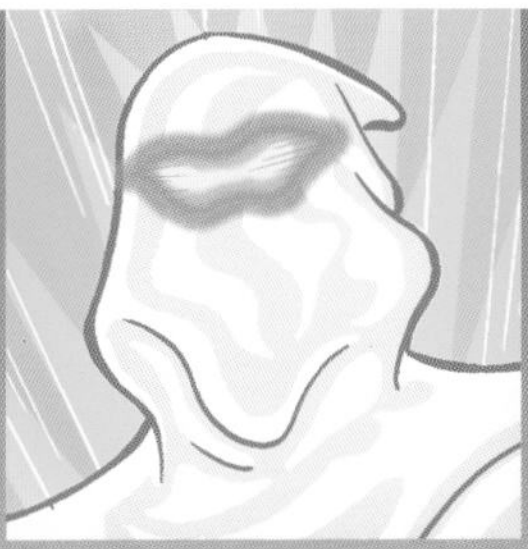

Dr Avatar,
Jonnie's mentor
from outer space

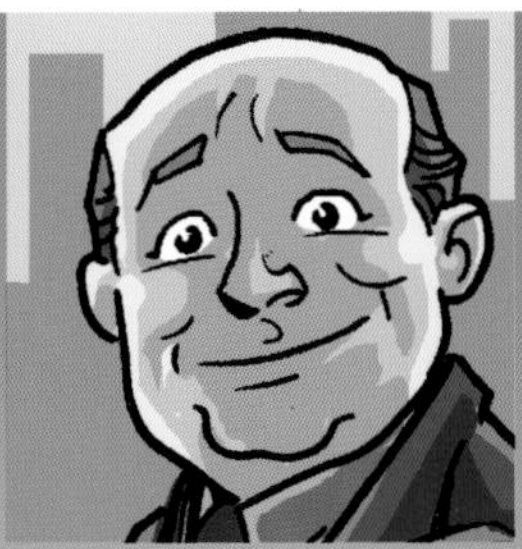

Kenneth,
the bus
driver

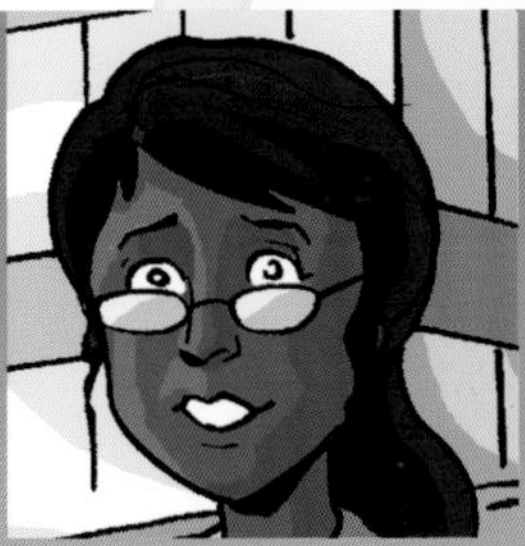

Sophia,
Jonnie's best
friend

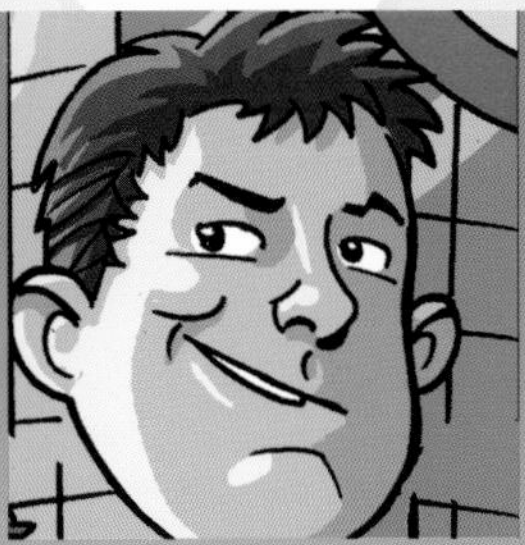

Briar Baz,
gang
leader

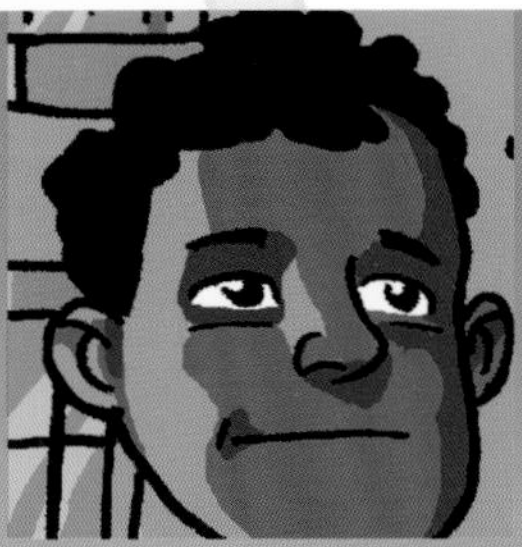

Charlie,
gang
member

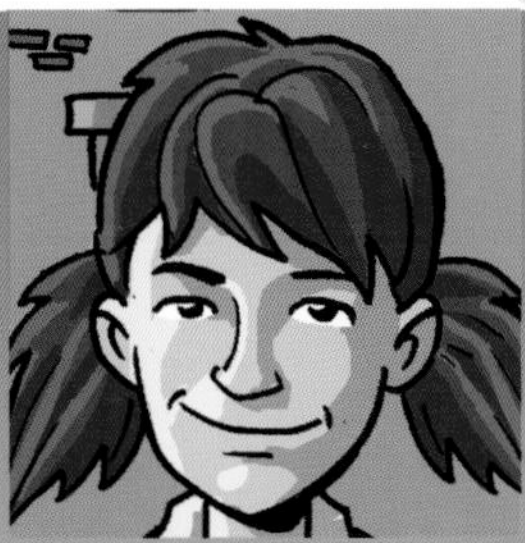

Vanessa,
gang
member

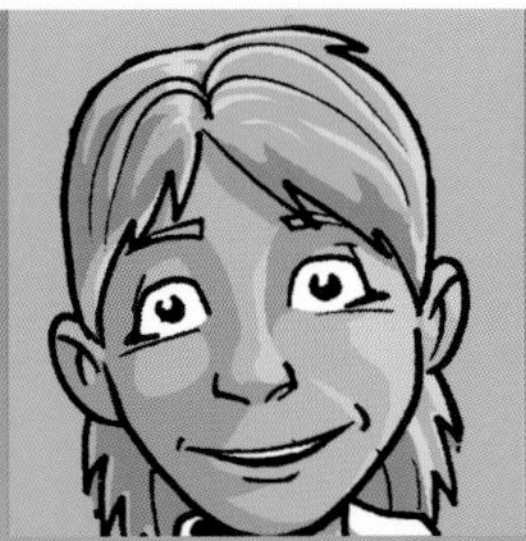

Charlotte,
passenger on
the bus

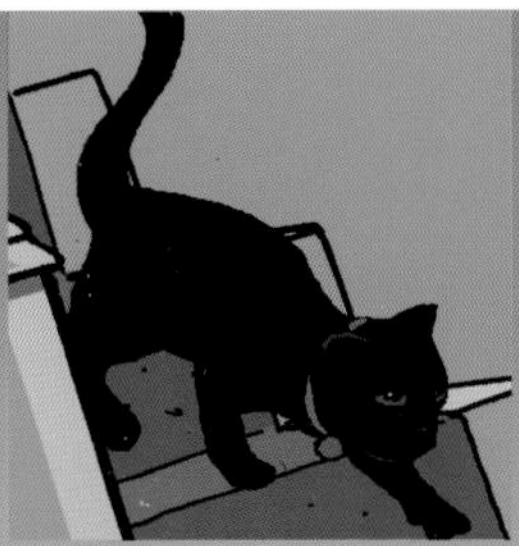

Captain Flinty,
Jonnie's cat

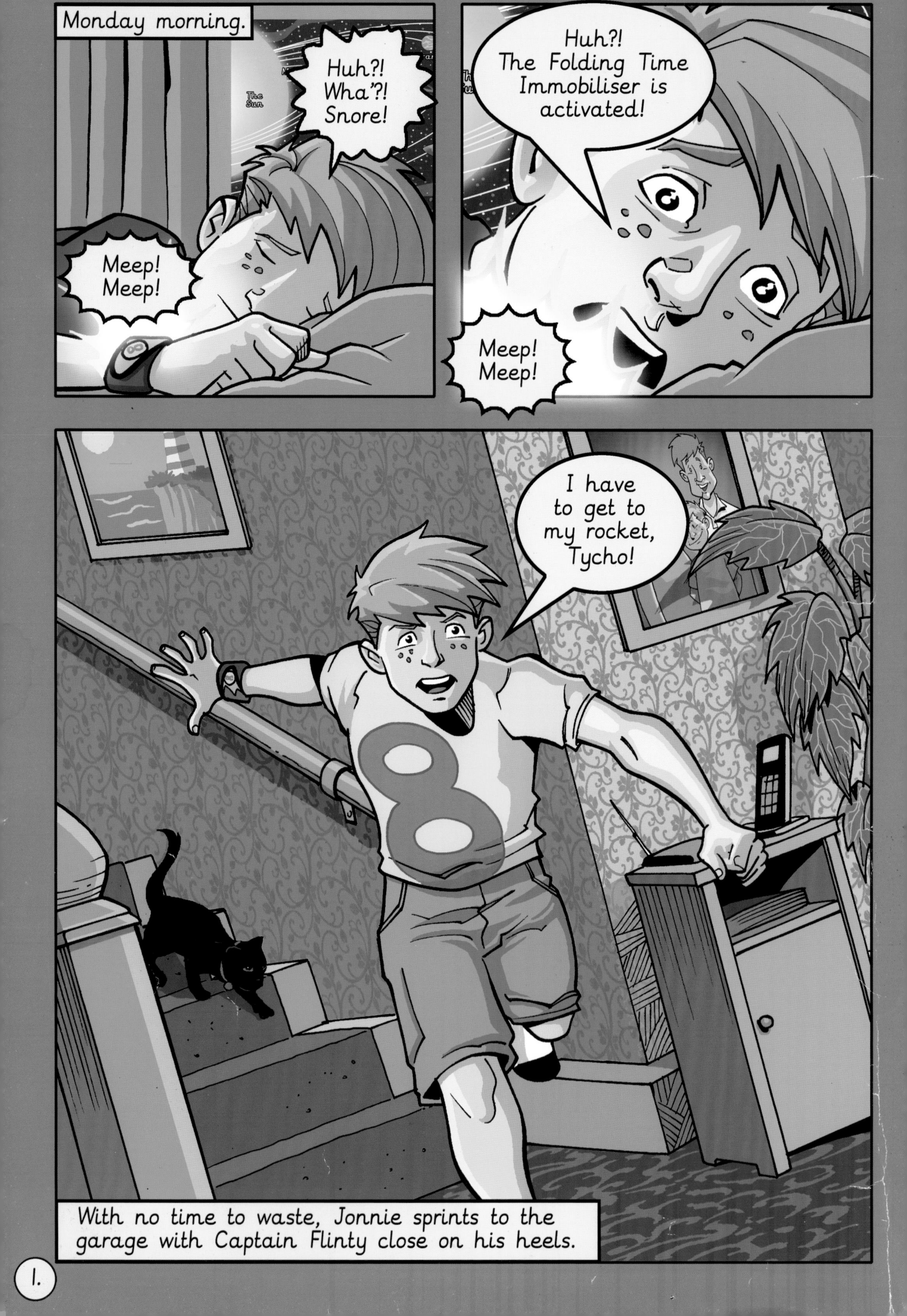
Monday morning.
Huh?! Wha'?! Snore!
Meep! Meep!
Huh?! The Folding Time Immobiliser is activated!
Meep! Meep!
I have to get to my rocket, Tycho!
With no time to waste, Jonnie sprints to the garage with Captain Flinty close on his heels.

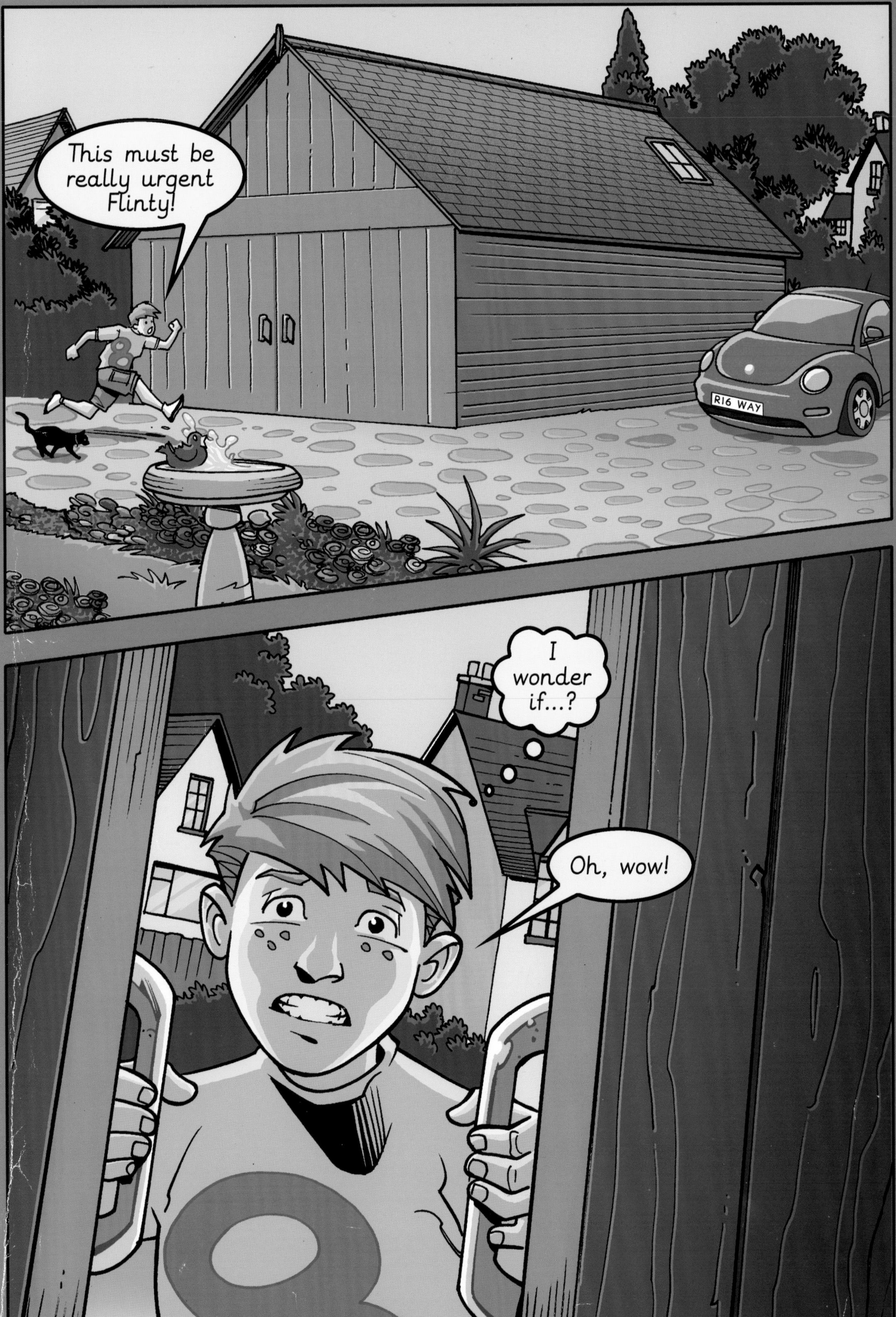
This must be really urgent Flinty!
R16 WAY
I wonder if...?
Oh, wow!

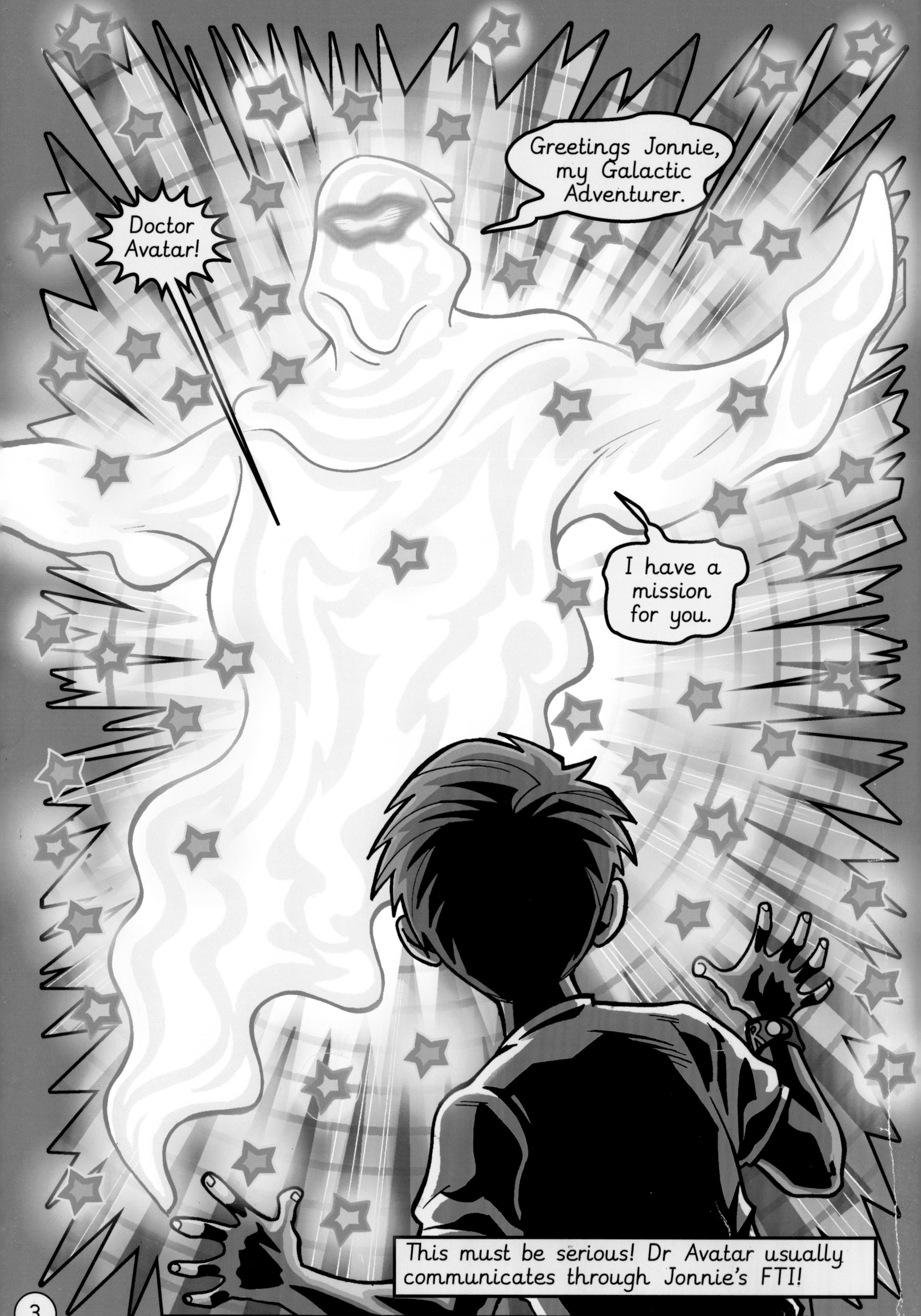
Doctor Avatar!
Greetings Jonnie, my Galactic Adventurer.
I have a mission for you.
This must be serious! Dr Avatar usually communicates through Jonnie's FTI!

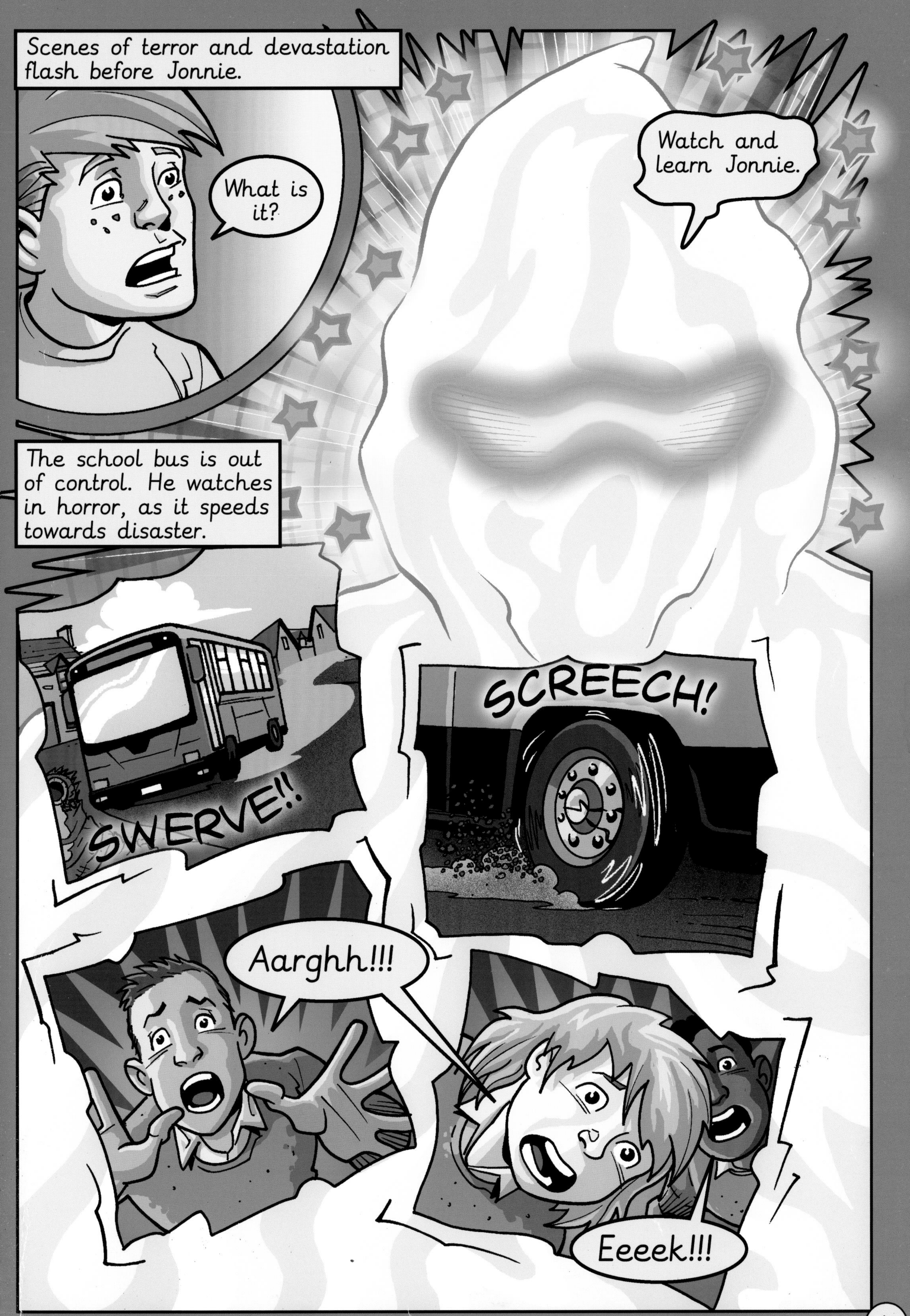
Scenes of terror and devastation flash before Jonnie.
What is it?
Watch and learn Jonnie.
The school bus is out of control. He watches in horror, as it speeds towards disaster.
SWERVE!!
SCREECH!
Aarghh!!!
Eeeek!!!

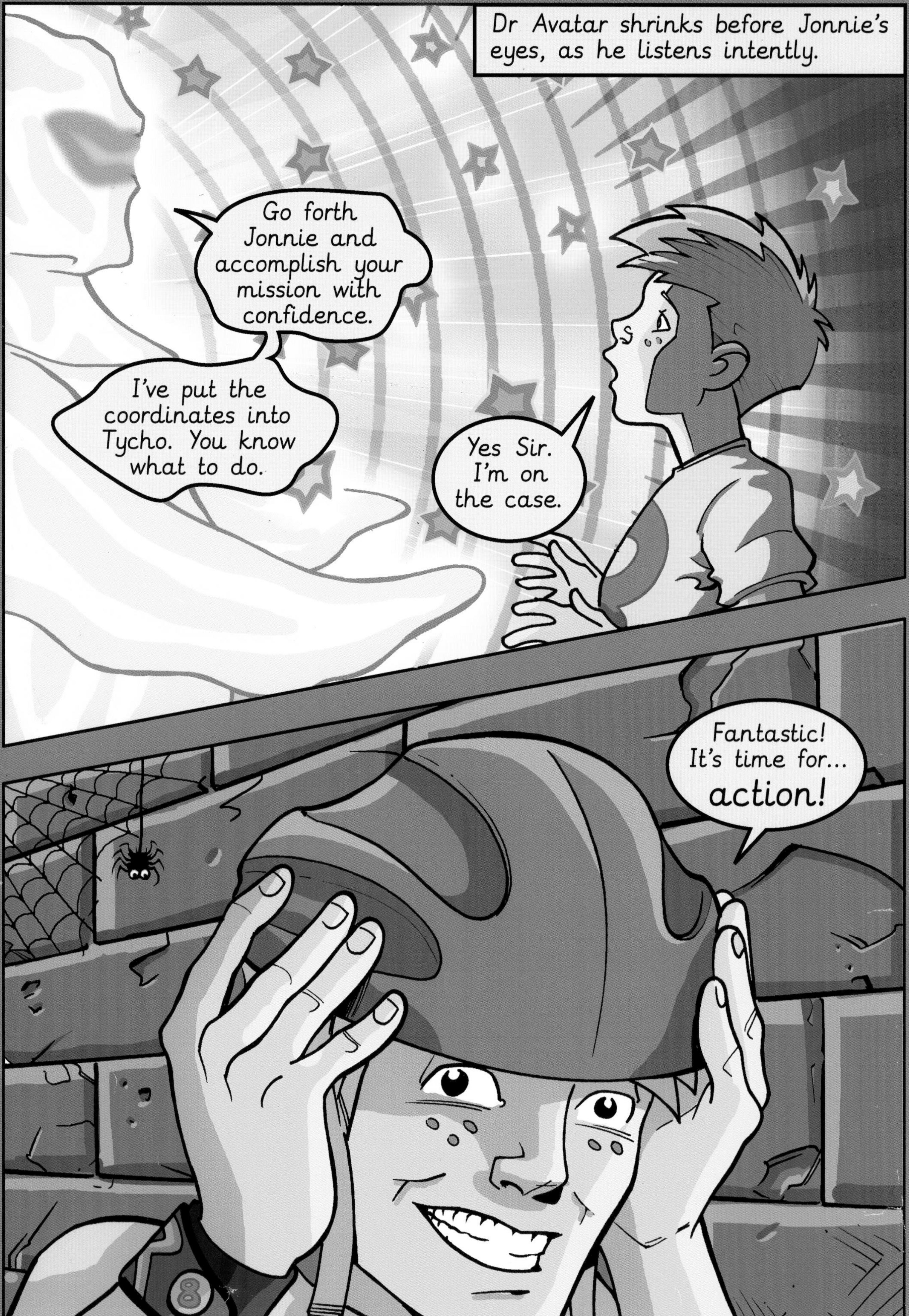
Dr Avatar shrinks before Jonnie's eyes, as he listens intently.
Go forth Jonnie and accomplish your mission with confidence.
I've put the coordinates into Tycho. You know what to do.
Yes Sir. I'm on the case.
Fantastic! It's time for... action!
Dr Avatar vaporizes as Jonnie prepares for his mission with both excitement and trepidation.

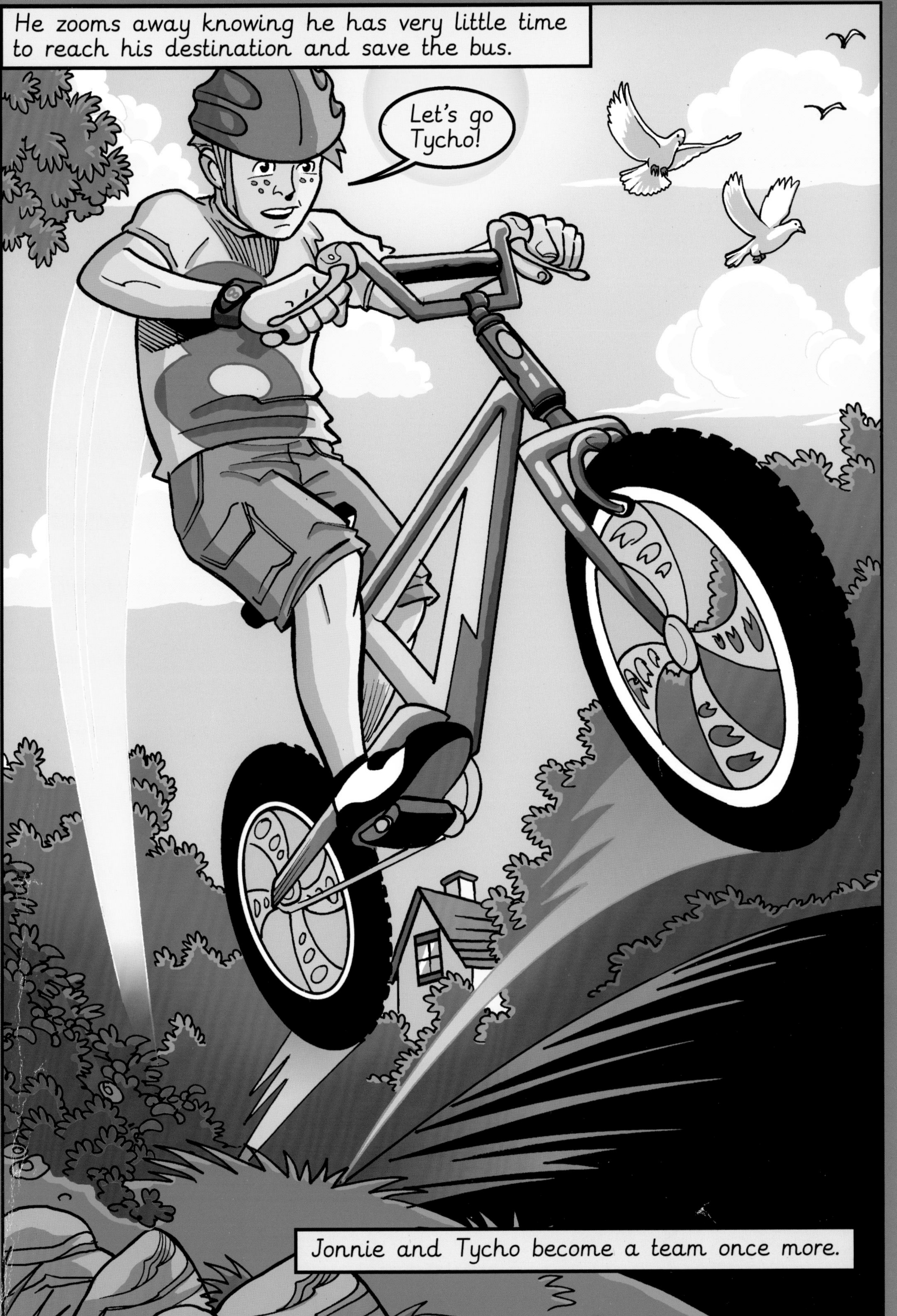
He zooms away knowing he has very little time to reach his destination and save the bus.
Let's go Tycho!
Jonnie and Tycho become a team once more.

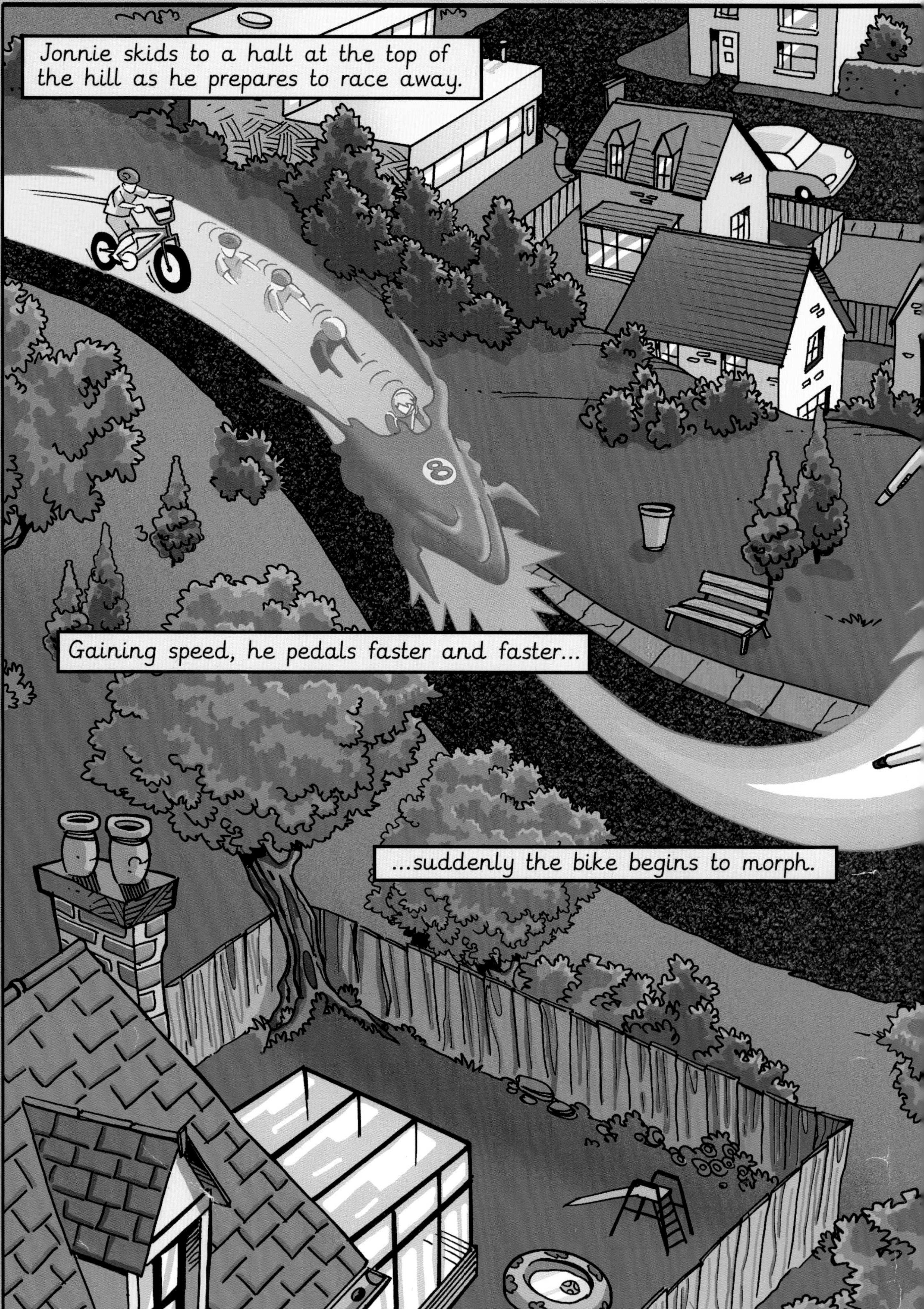
Jonnie skids to a halt at the top of the hill as he prepares to race away.
Gaining speed, he pedals faster and faster...
...suddenly the bike begins to morph.

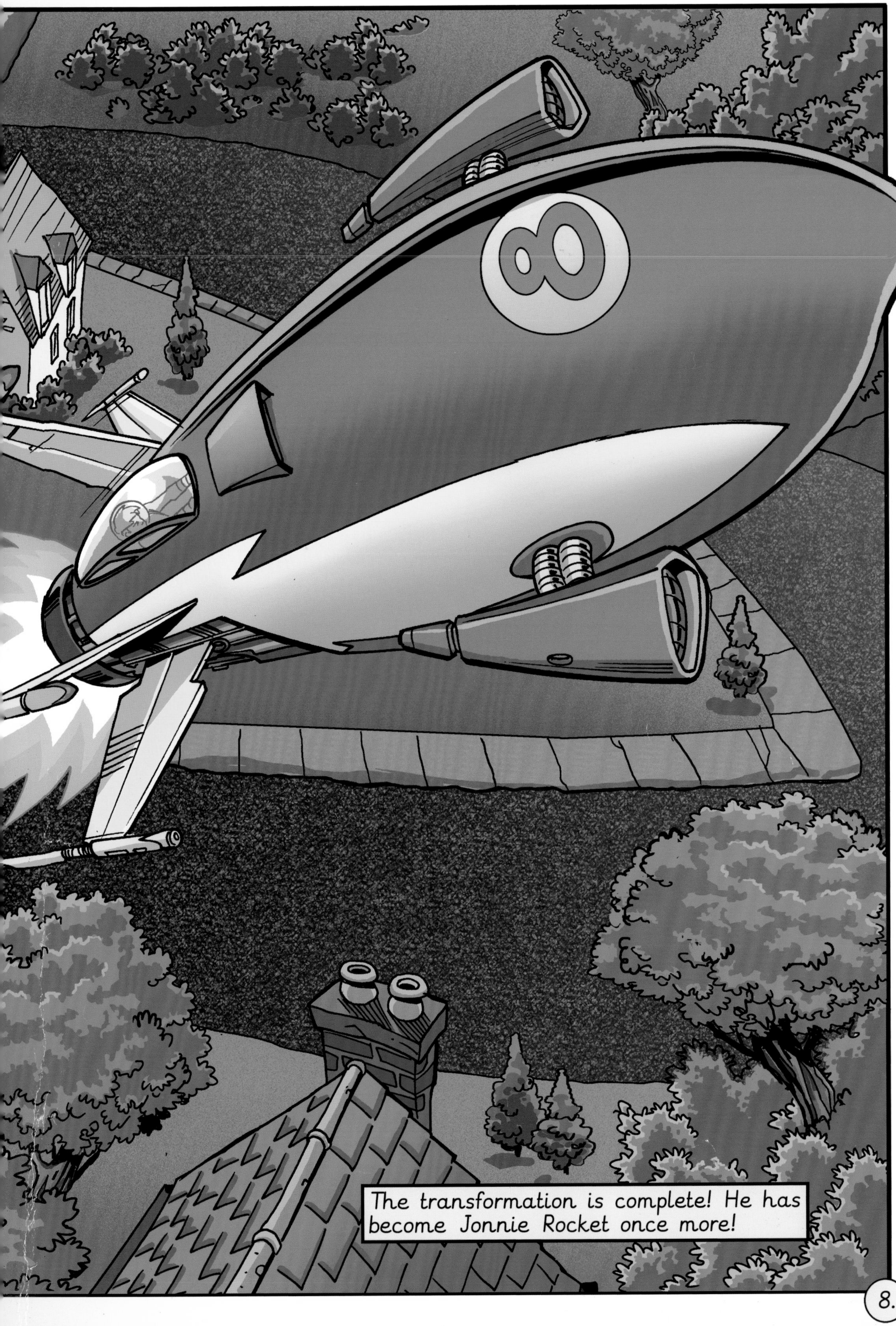
The transformation is complete! He has become Jonnie Rocket once more!

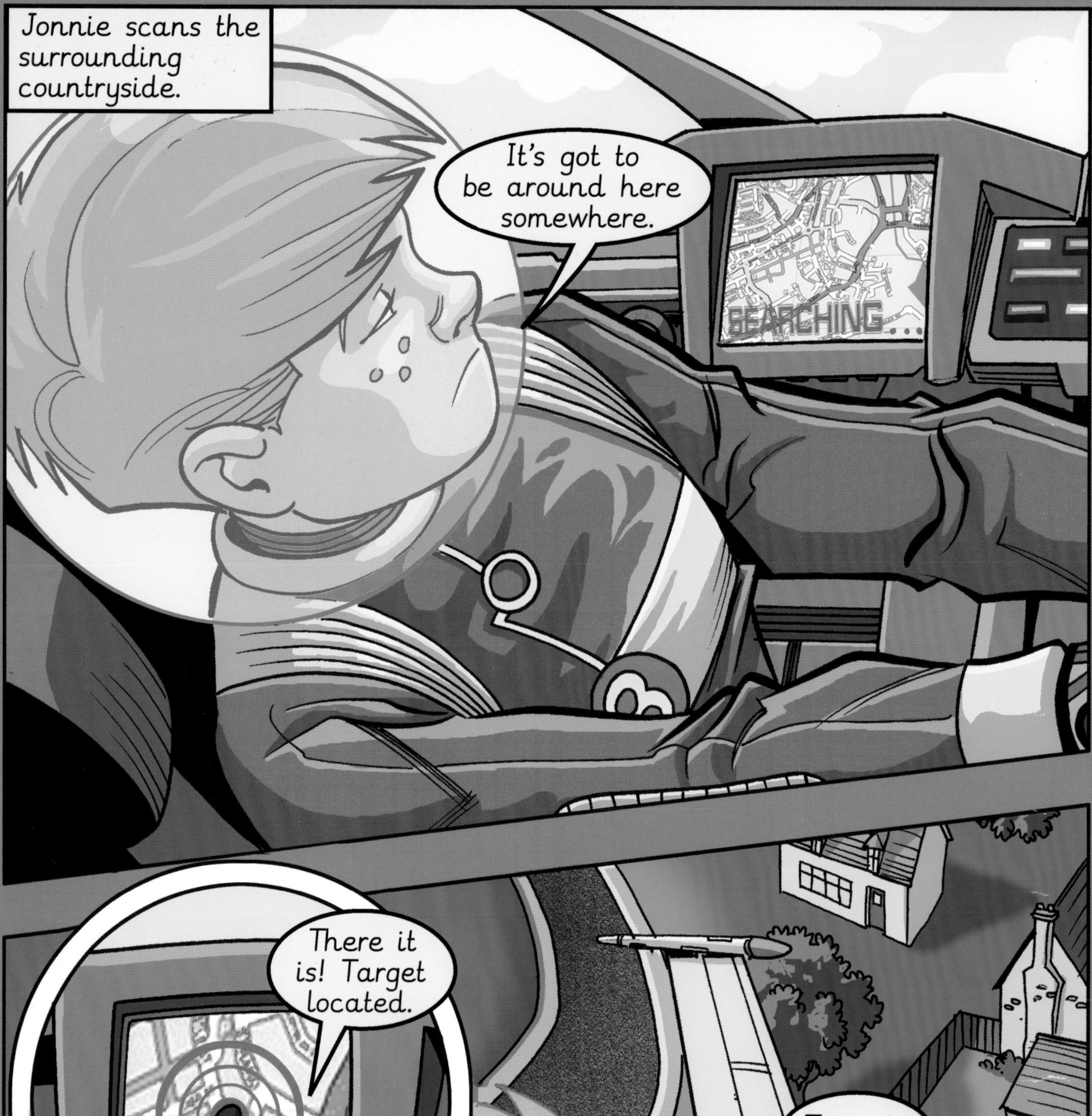
Jonnie scans the surrounding countryside.
It's got to be around here somewhere.
SEARCHING...

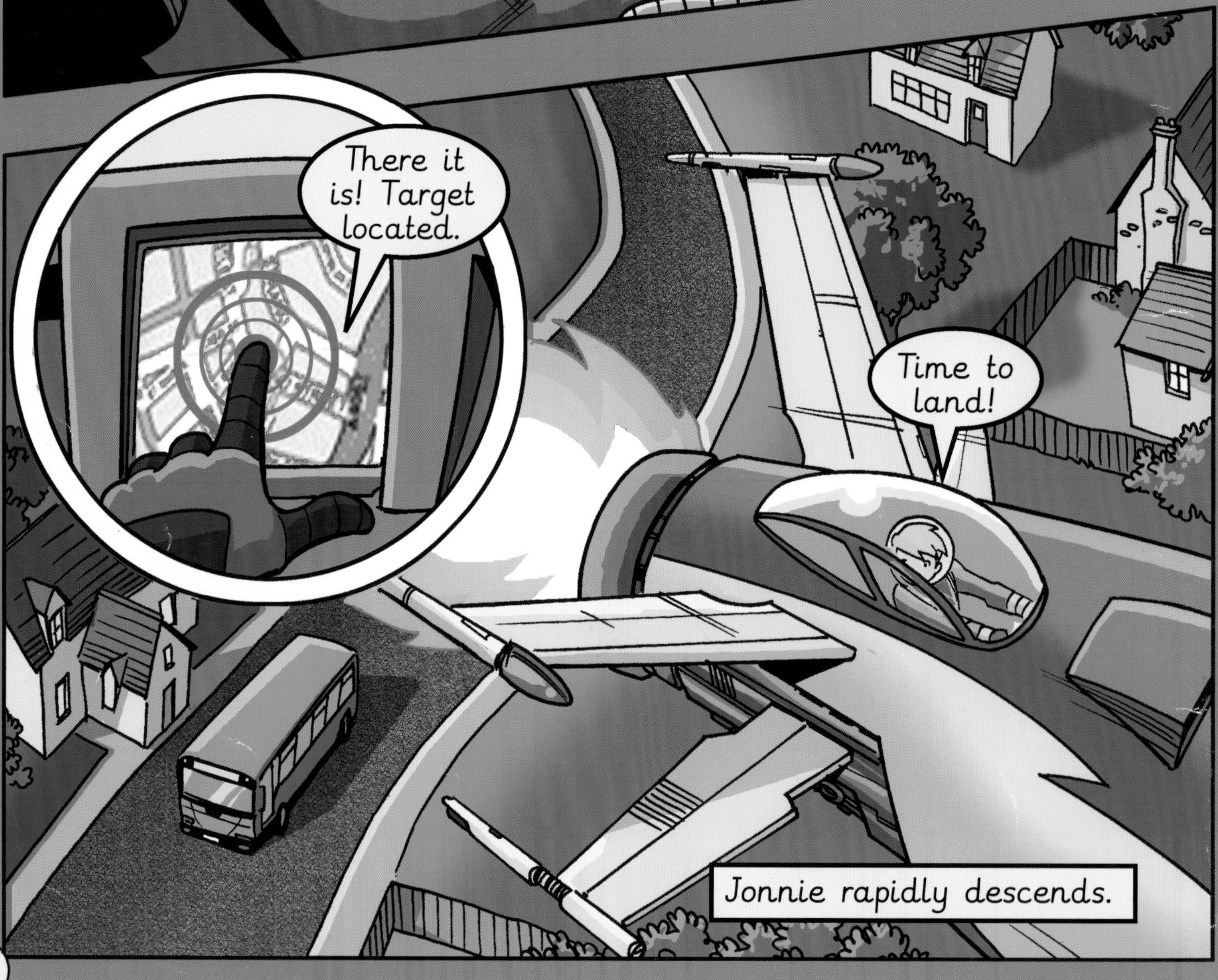
There it is! Target located.
Time to land!
Jonnie rapidly descends.

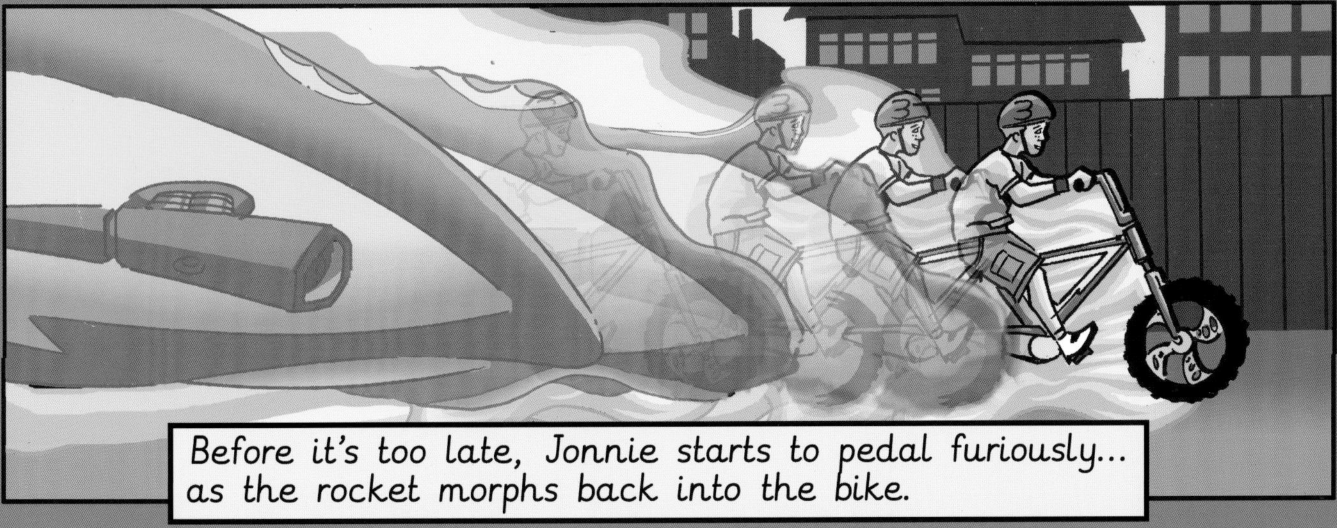
Before it's too late, Jonnie starts to pedal furiously...
as the rocket morphs back into the bike.

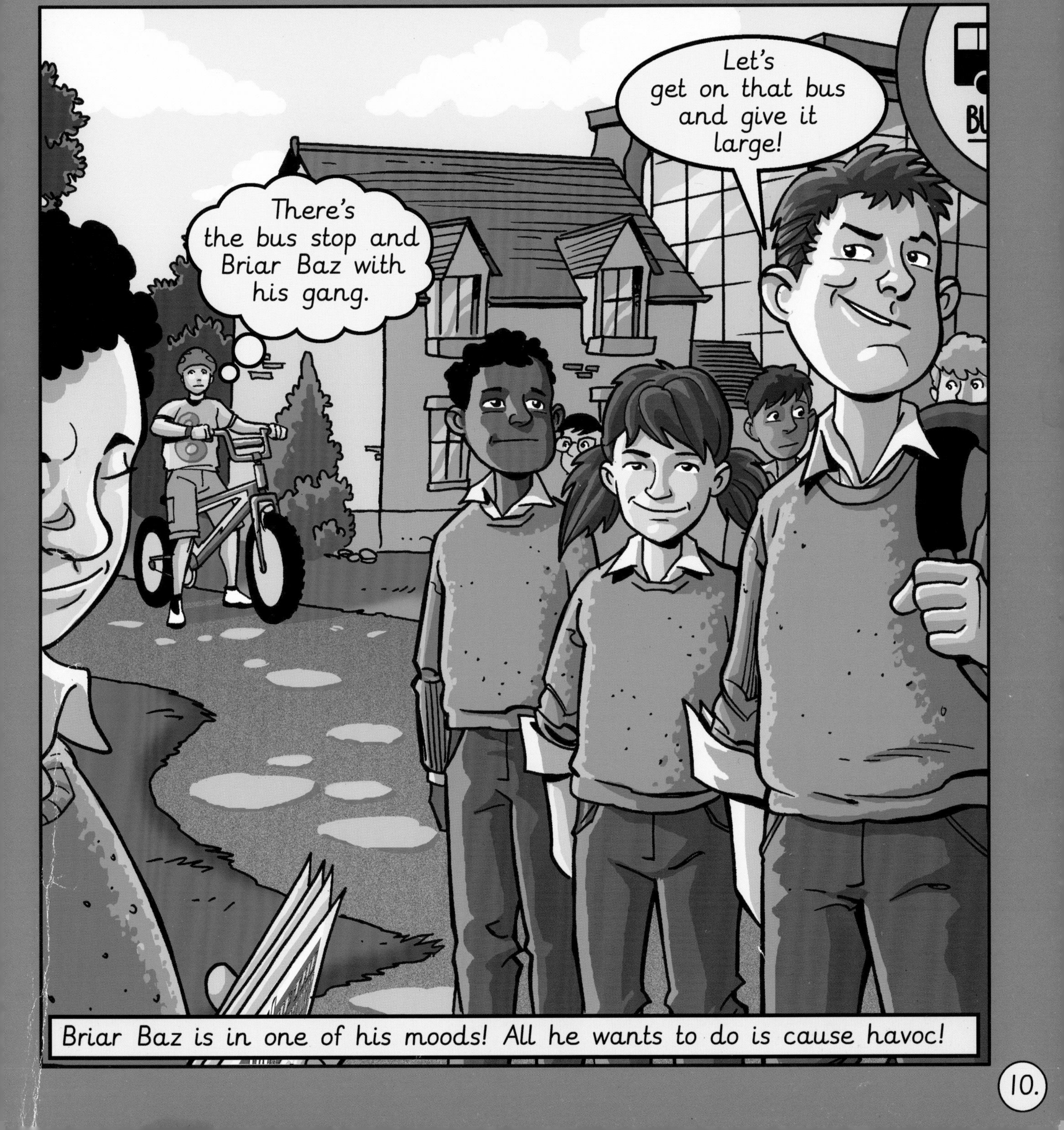
There's the bus stop and Briar Baz with his gang.
Let's get on that bus and give it large!
Briar Baz is in one of his moods! All he wants to do is cause havoc!

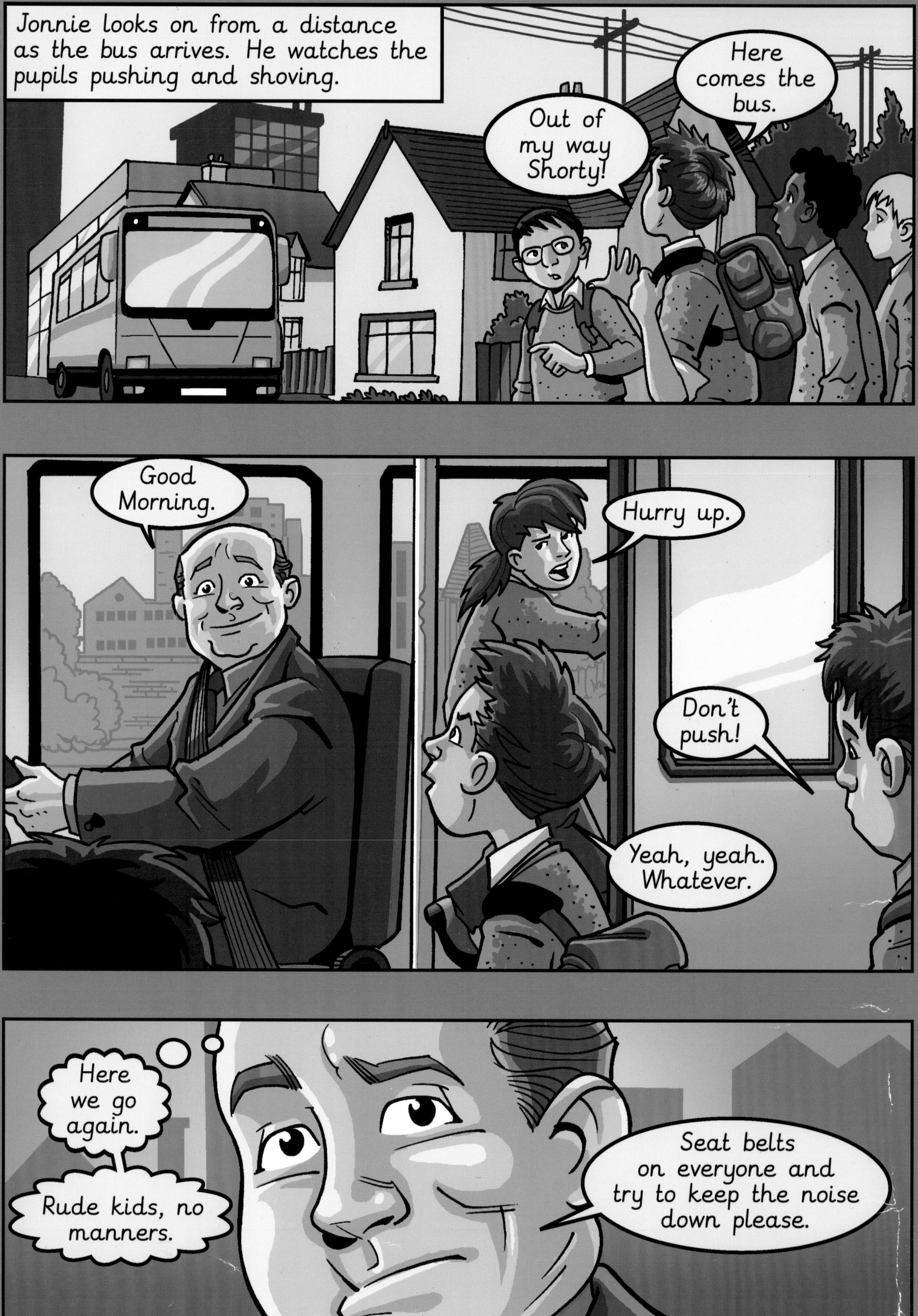
Jonnie looks on from a distance as the bus arrives. He watches the pupils pushing and shoving.
Out of my way Shorty!
Here comes the bus.
Good Morning.
Hurry up.
Don't push!
Yeah, yeah. Whatever.
Here we go again.
Rude kids, no manners.
Seat belts on everyone and try to keep the noise down please.
Every day Ken tries to be friendly and pleasant... but little does he know that this trip will end in disaster!!

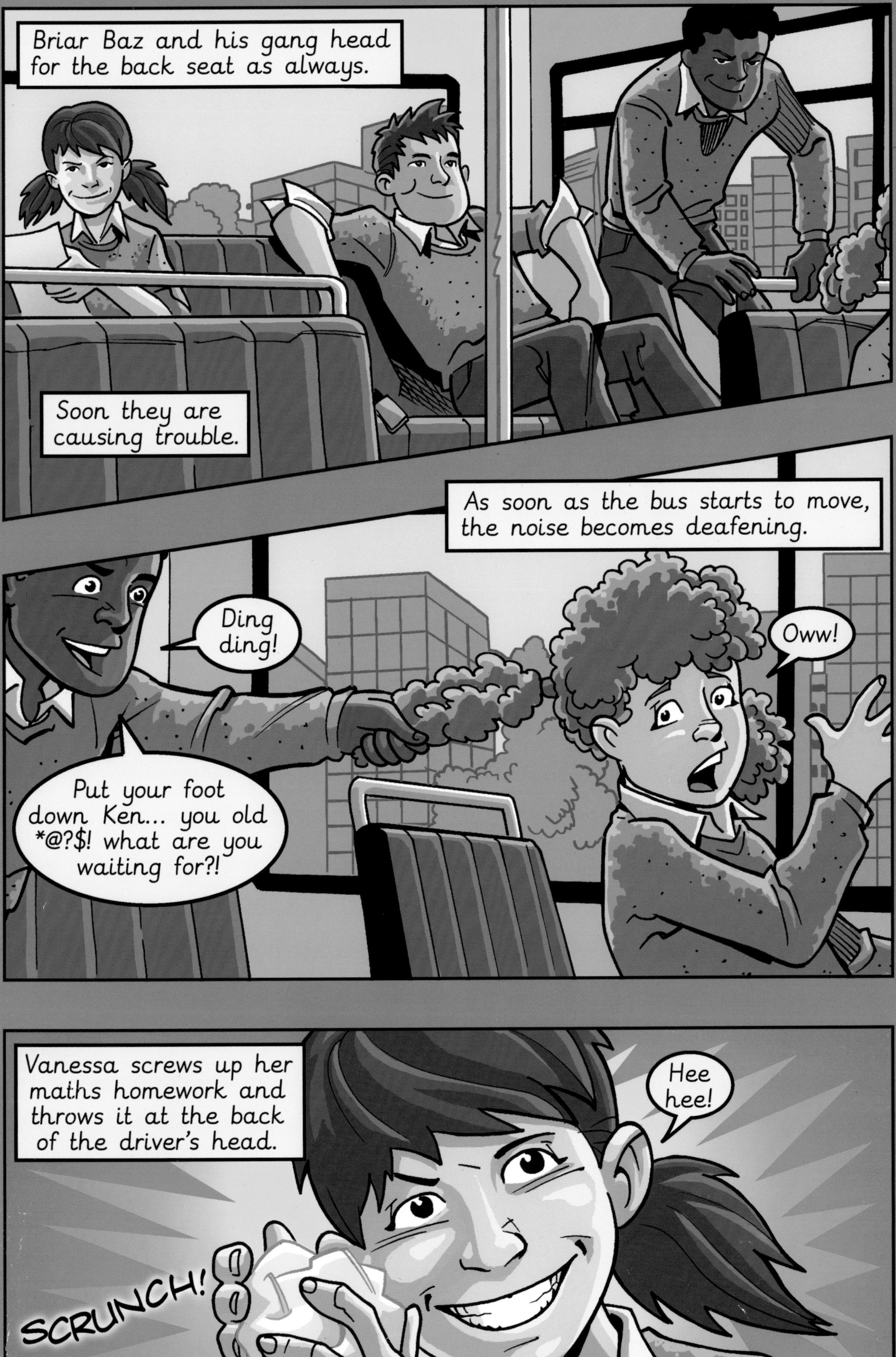
Briar Baz and his gang head for the back seat as always.
Soon they are causing trouble.
As soon as the bus starts to move, the noise becomes deafening.
Ding ding!
Put your foot down Ken... you old *@?$! what are you waiting for?!
Oww!
Vanessa screws up her maths homework and throws it at the back of the driver's head.
Hee hee!
SCRUNCH!

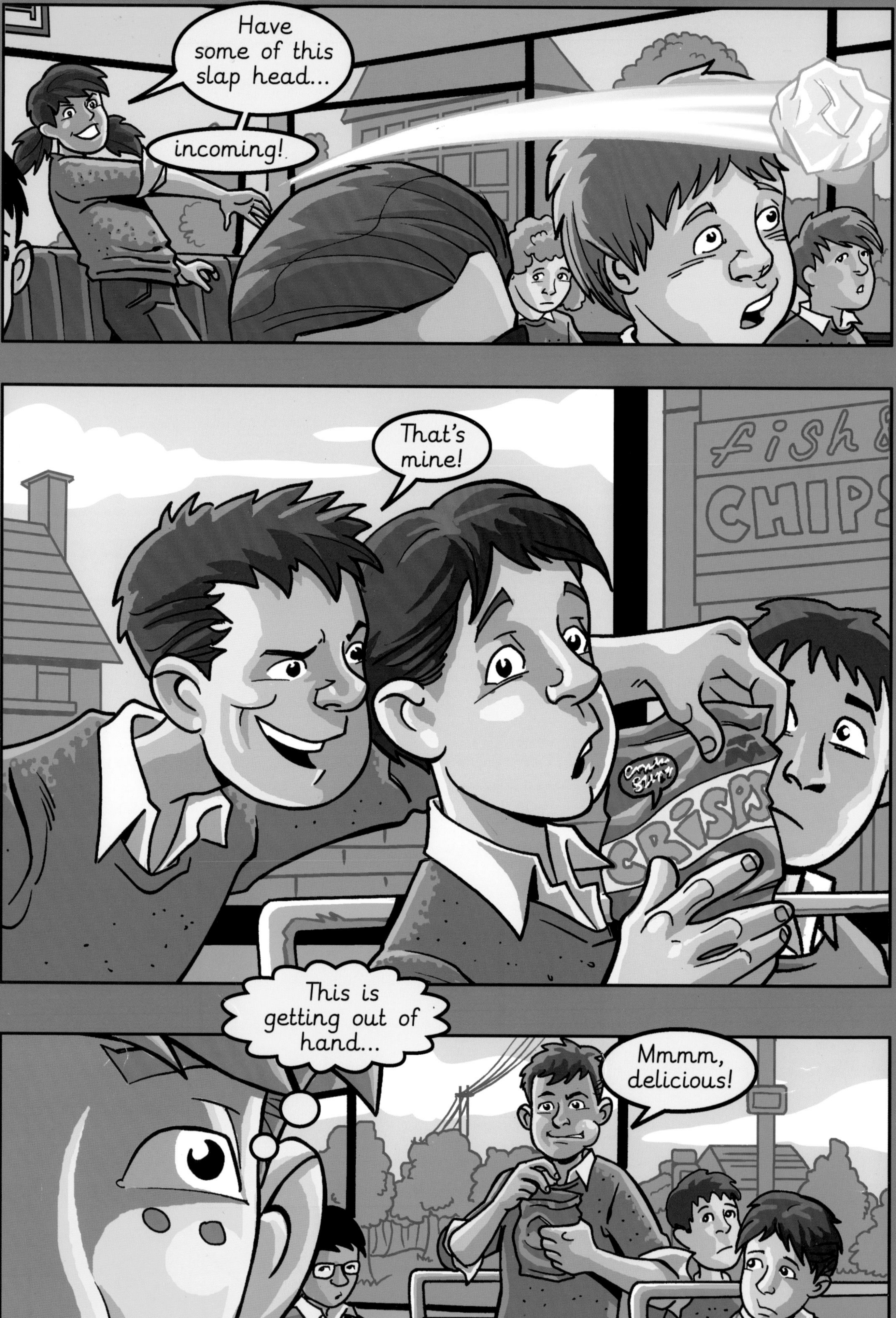
Have some of this slap head...
incoming!
That's mine!
CRISPS
This is getting out of hand...
Mmmm, delicious!

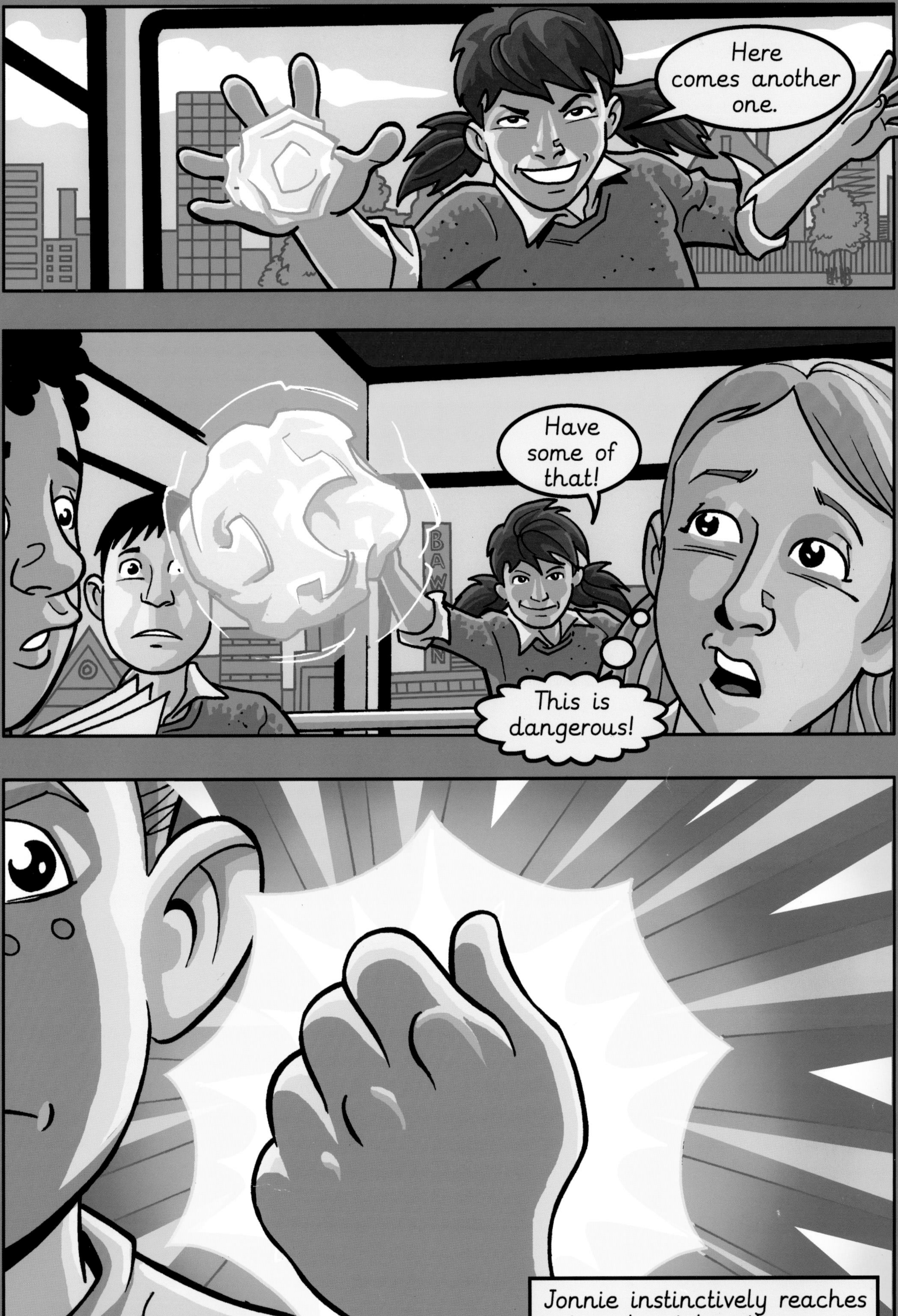
Here comes another one.
Have some of that!
This is dangerous!
Jonnie instinctively reaches out and catches the scrunched up paper ball.

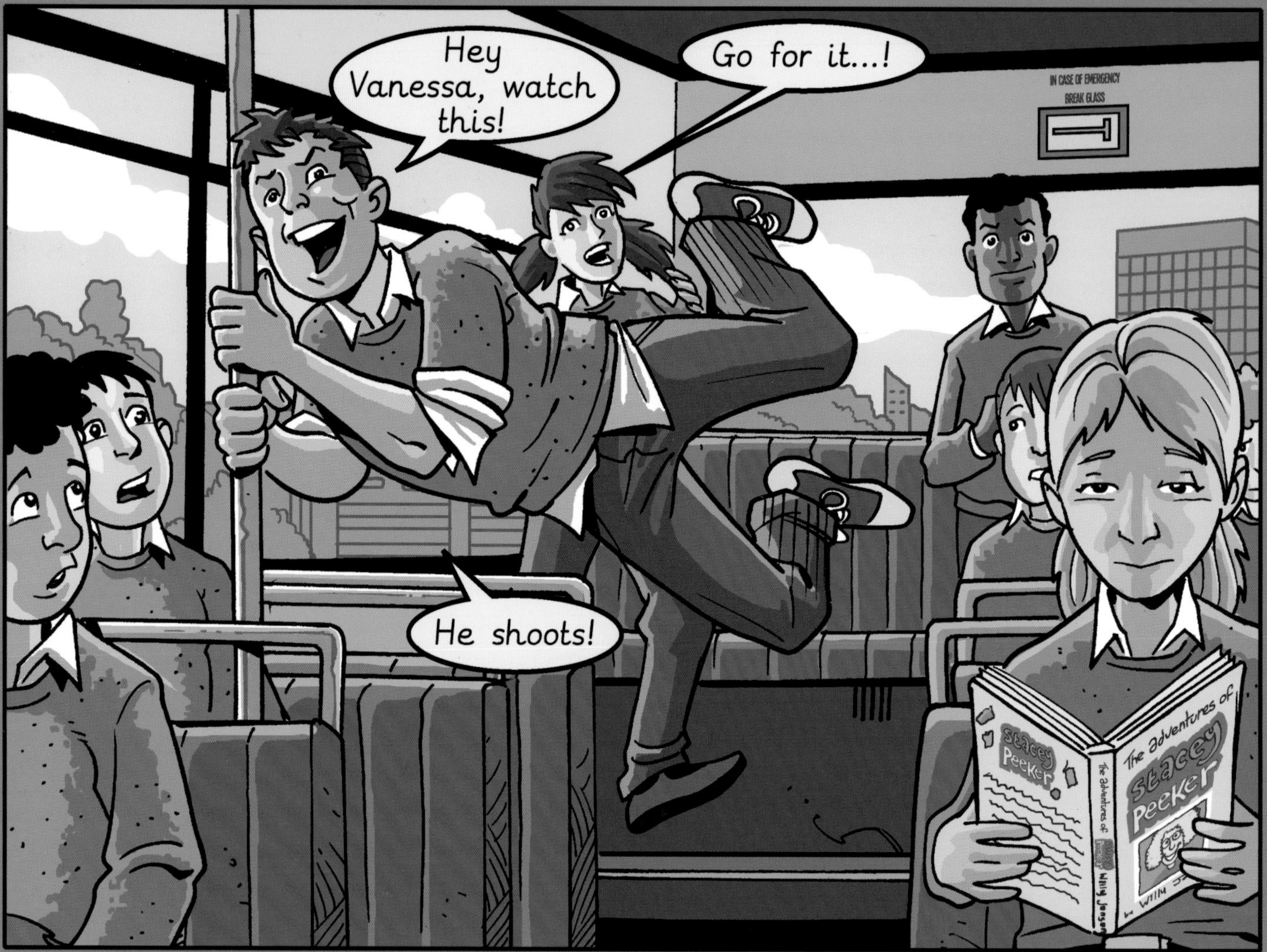
Hey Vanessa, watch this!
Go for it...!
IN CASE OF EMERGENCY
BREAK GLASS
He shoots!
The adventures of Stacey Peeker

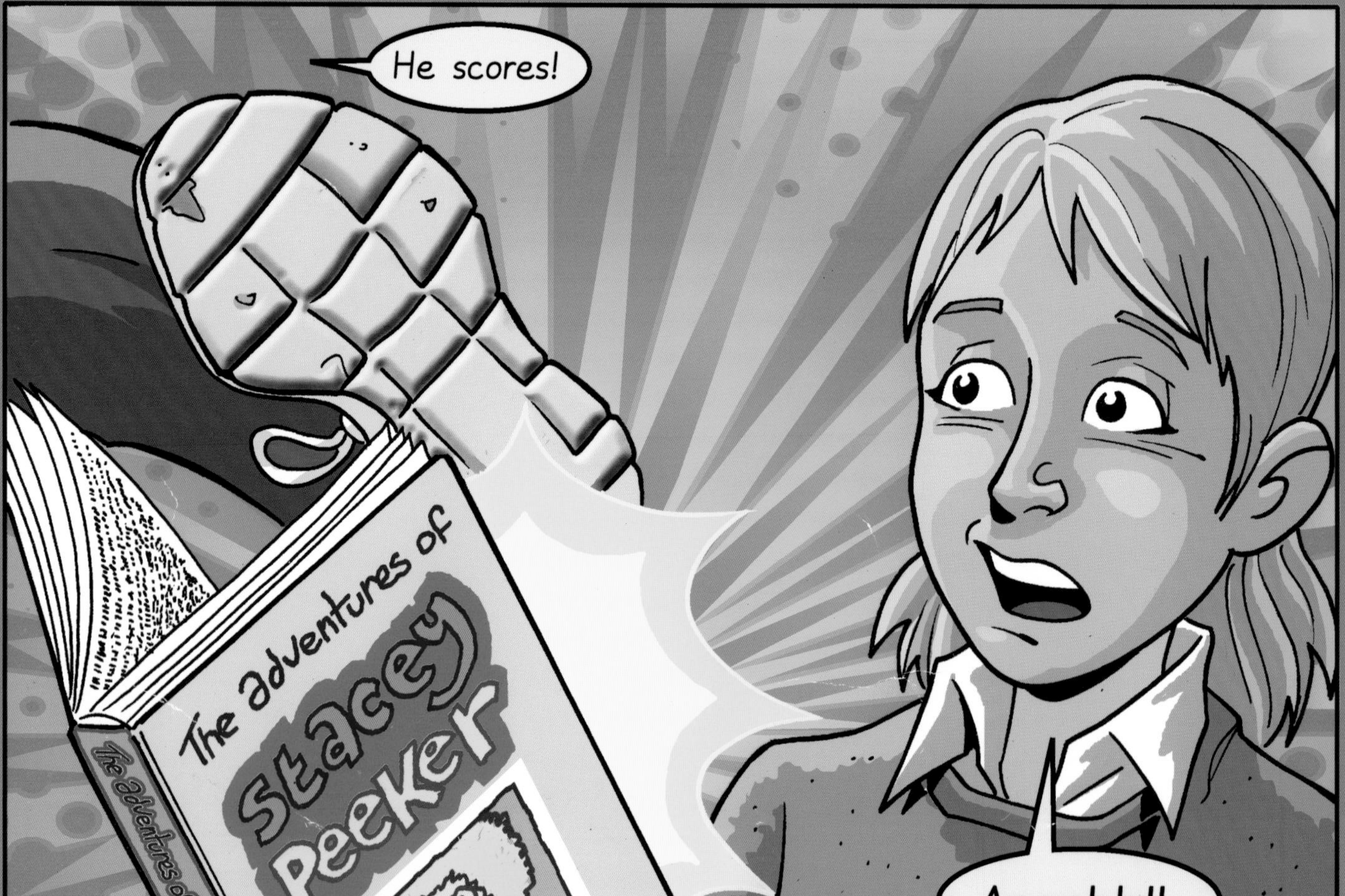
He scores!
The adventures of Stacey Peeker
Aaaahh!!

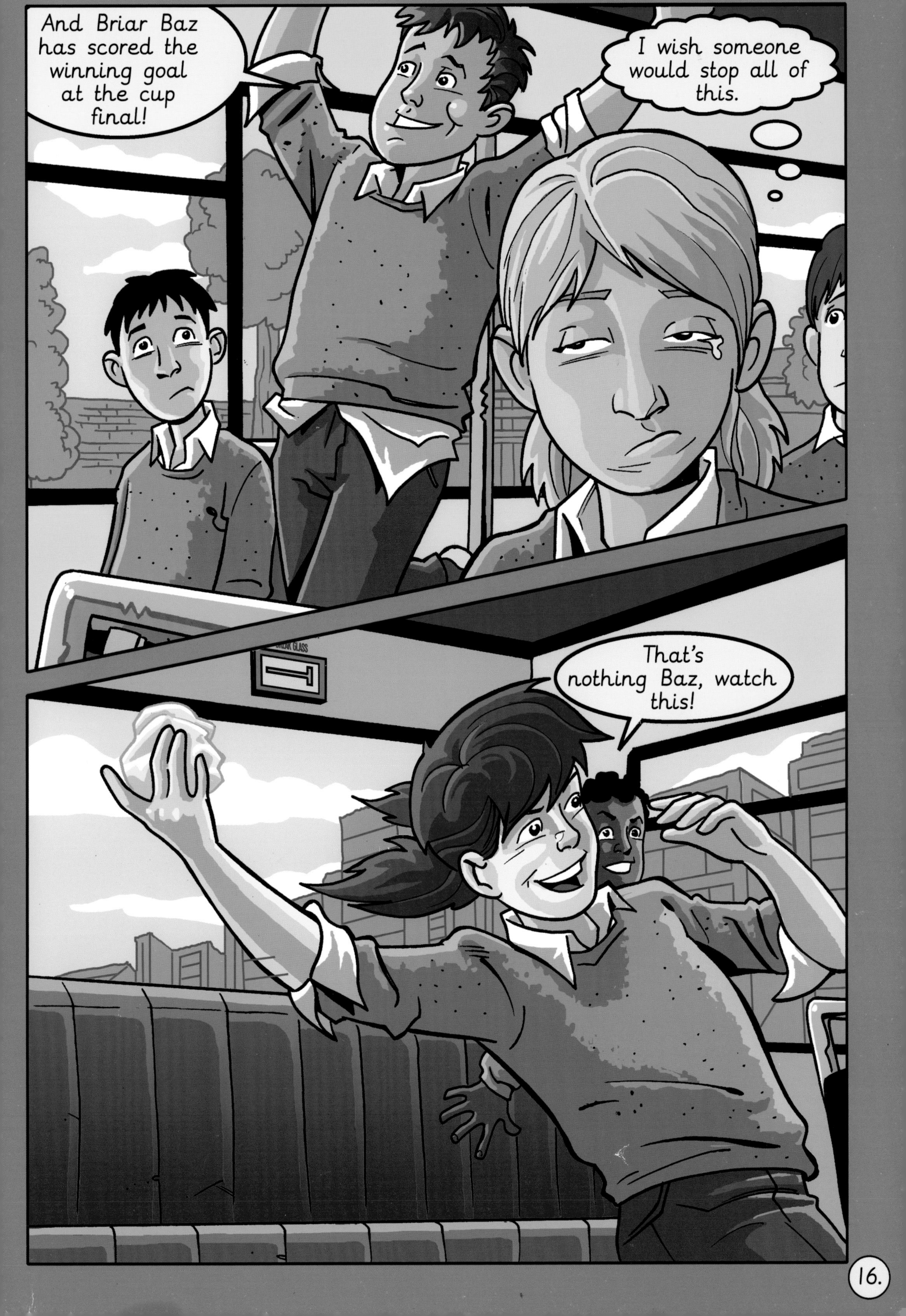
And Briar Baz has scored the winning goal at the cup final!
I wish someone would stop all of this.
That's nothing Baz, watch this!

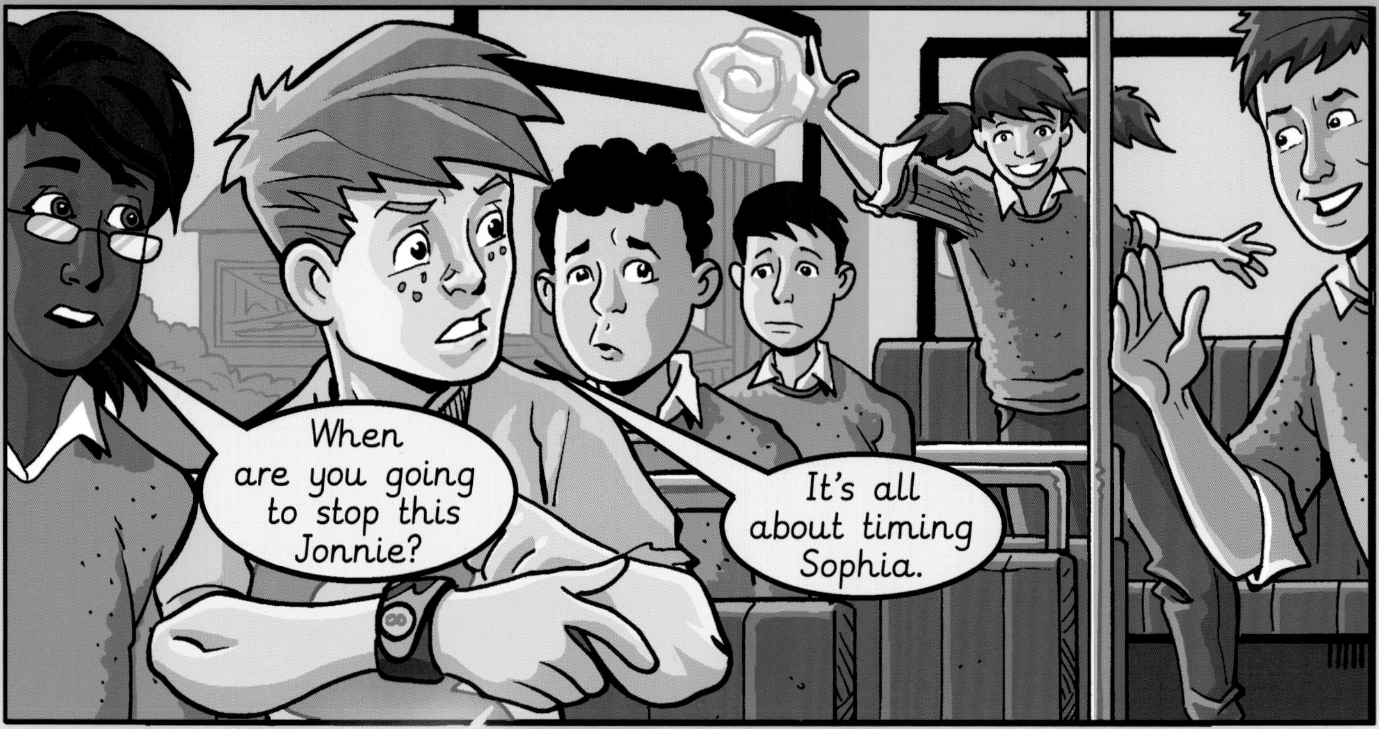
When are you going to stop this Jonnie?
It's all about timing Sophia.

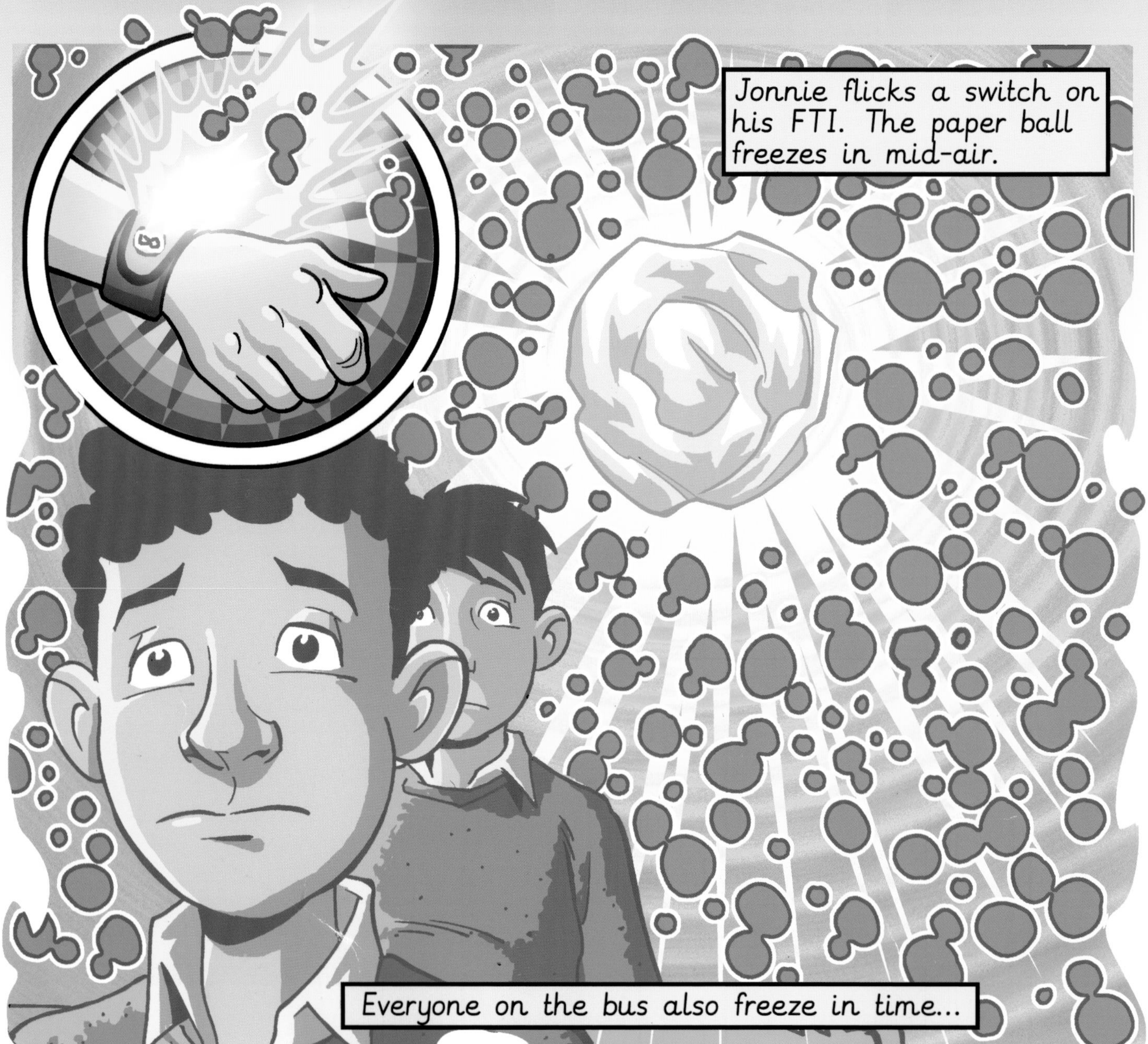
Jonnie flicks a switch on his FTI. The paper ball freezes in mid-air.
Everyone on the bus also freeze in time...

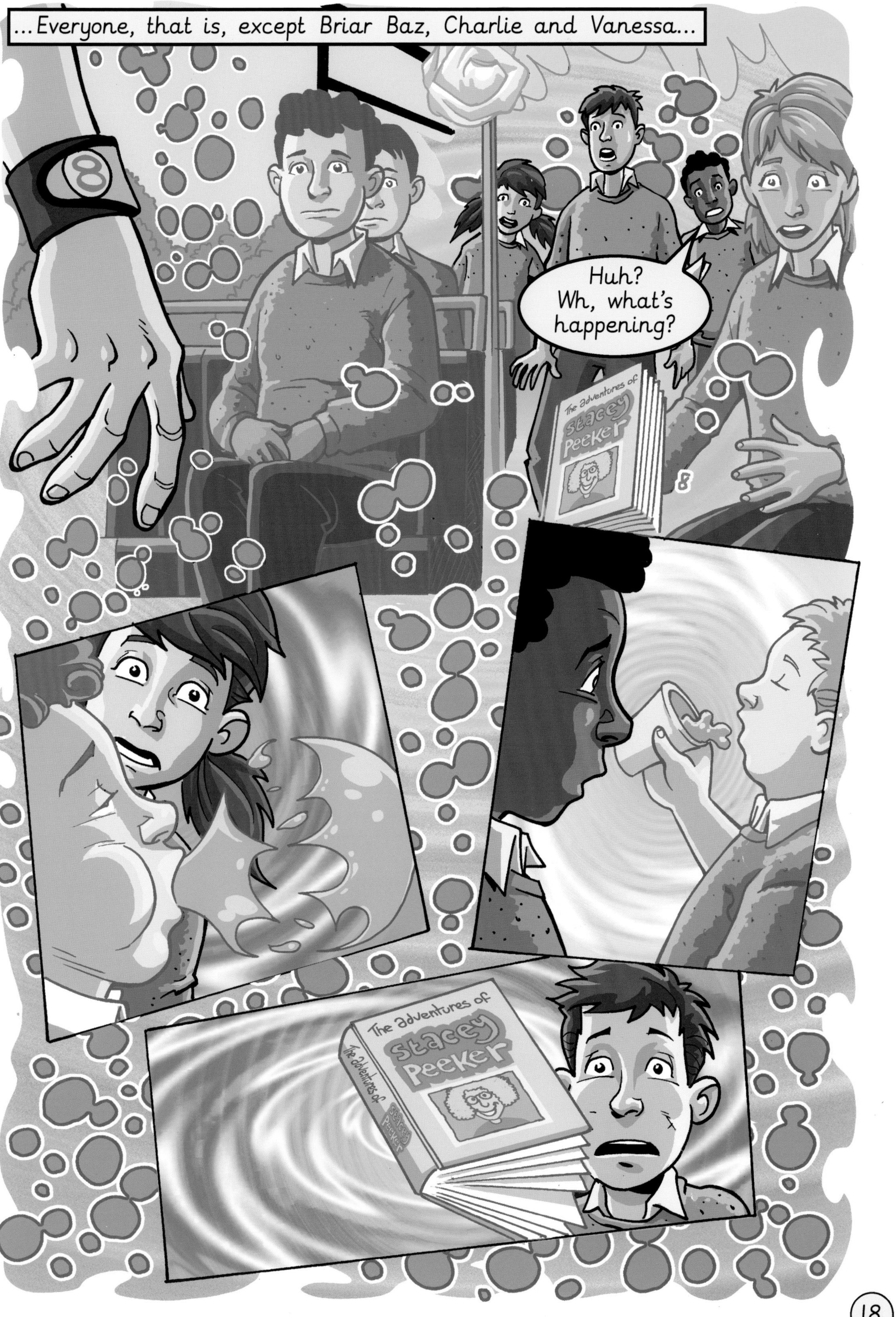
...Everyone, that is, except Briar Baz, Charlie and Vanessa...
Huh? Wh, what's happening?
The adventures of Stacey Peeker
The adventures of Stacey Peeker
The adventures of Stacey Peeker

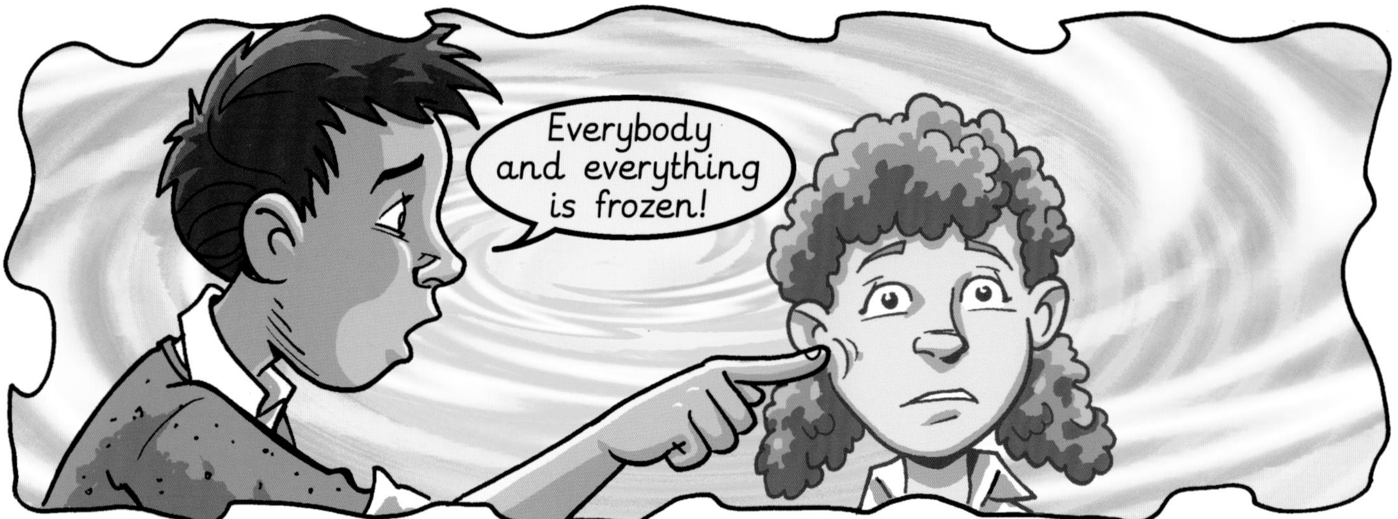
Everybody and everything is frozen!

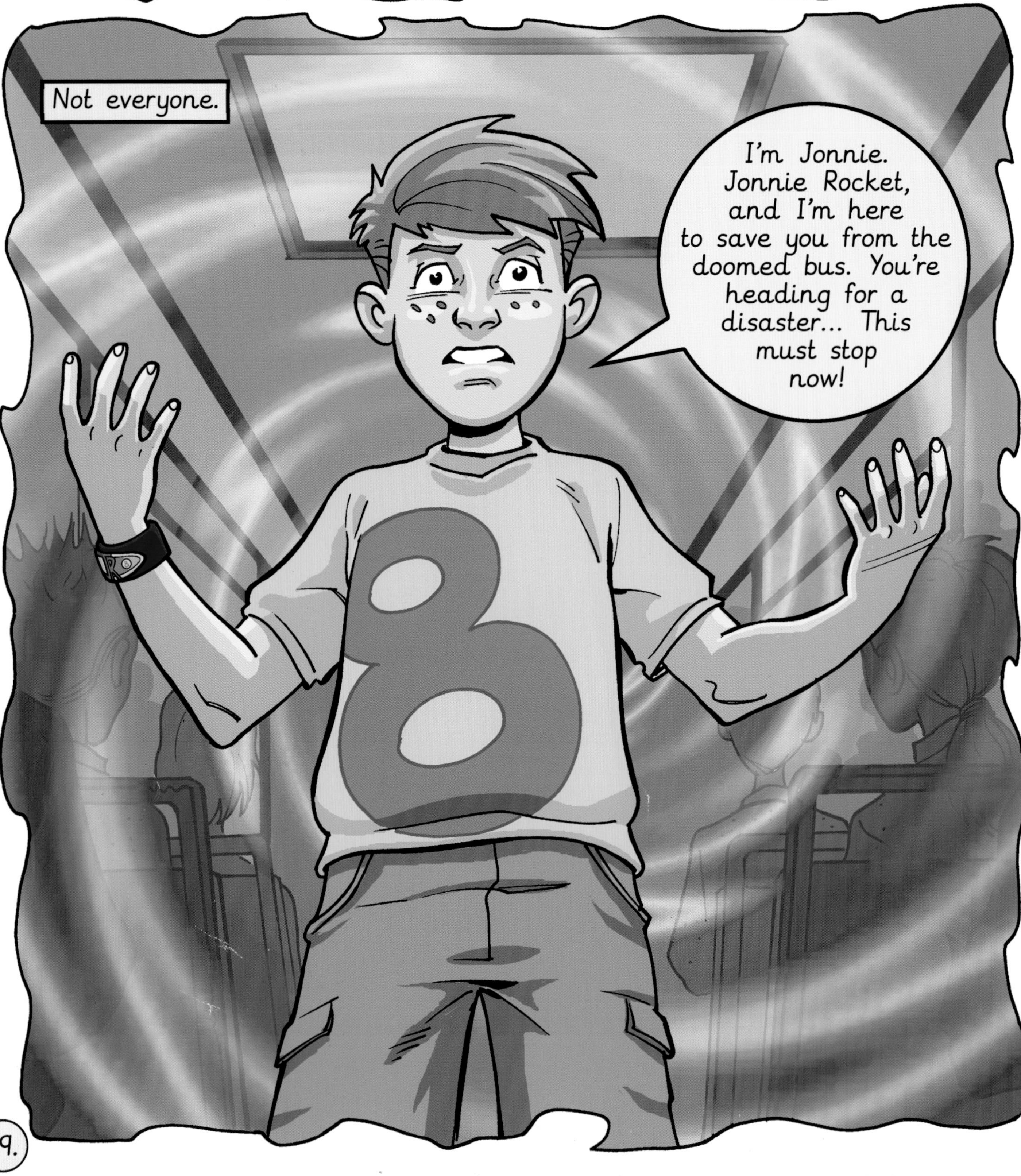
Not everyone.
I'm Jonnie. Jonnie Rocket, and I'm here to save you from the doomed bus. You're heading for a disaster... This must stop now!

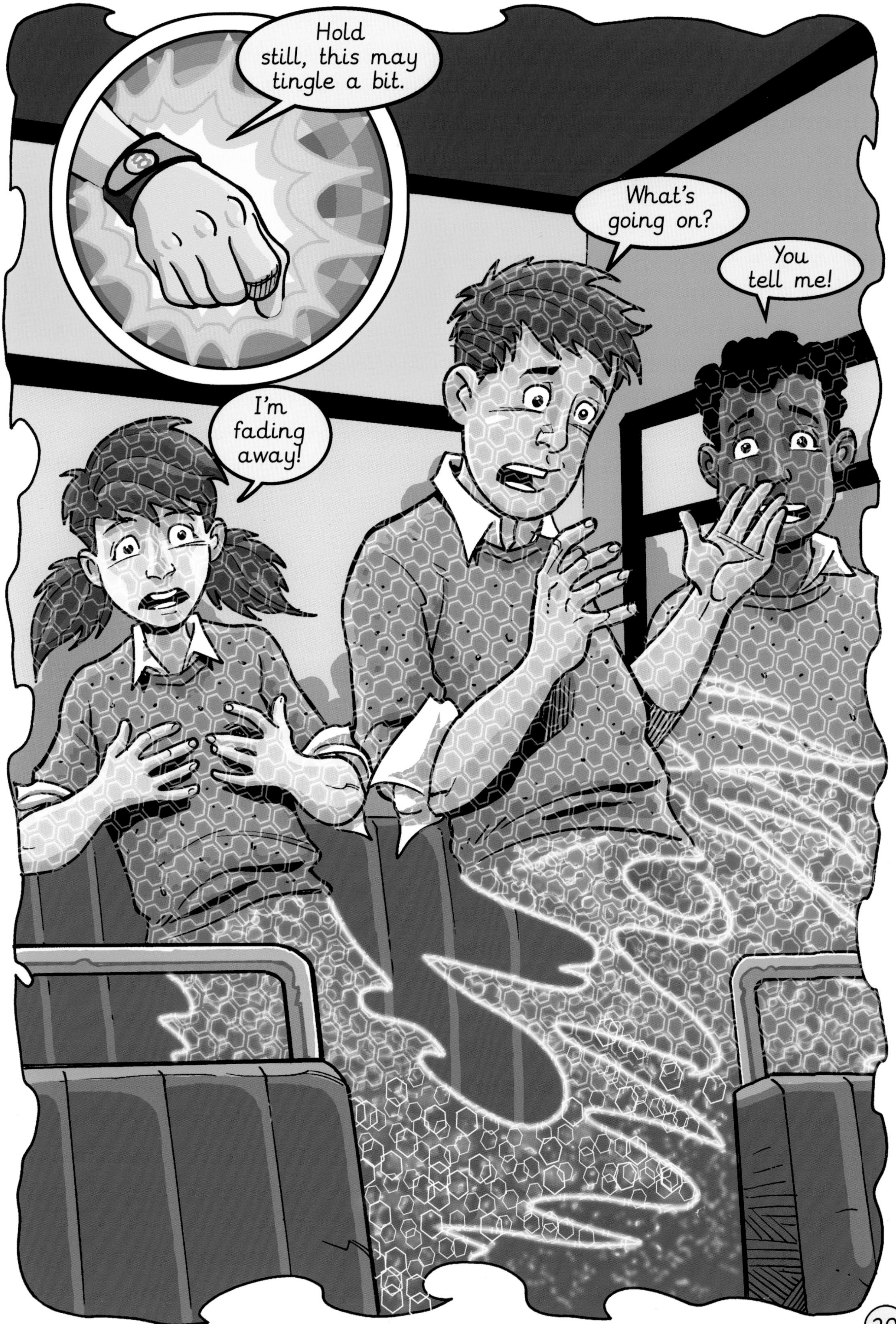
Hold still, this may tingle a bit.
What's going on?
You tell me!
I'm fading away!

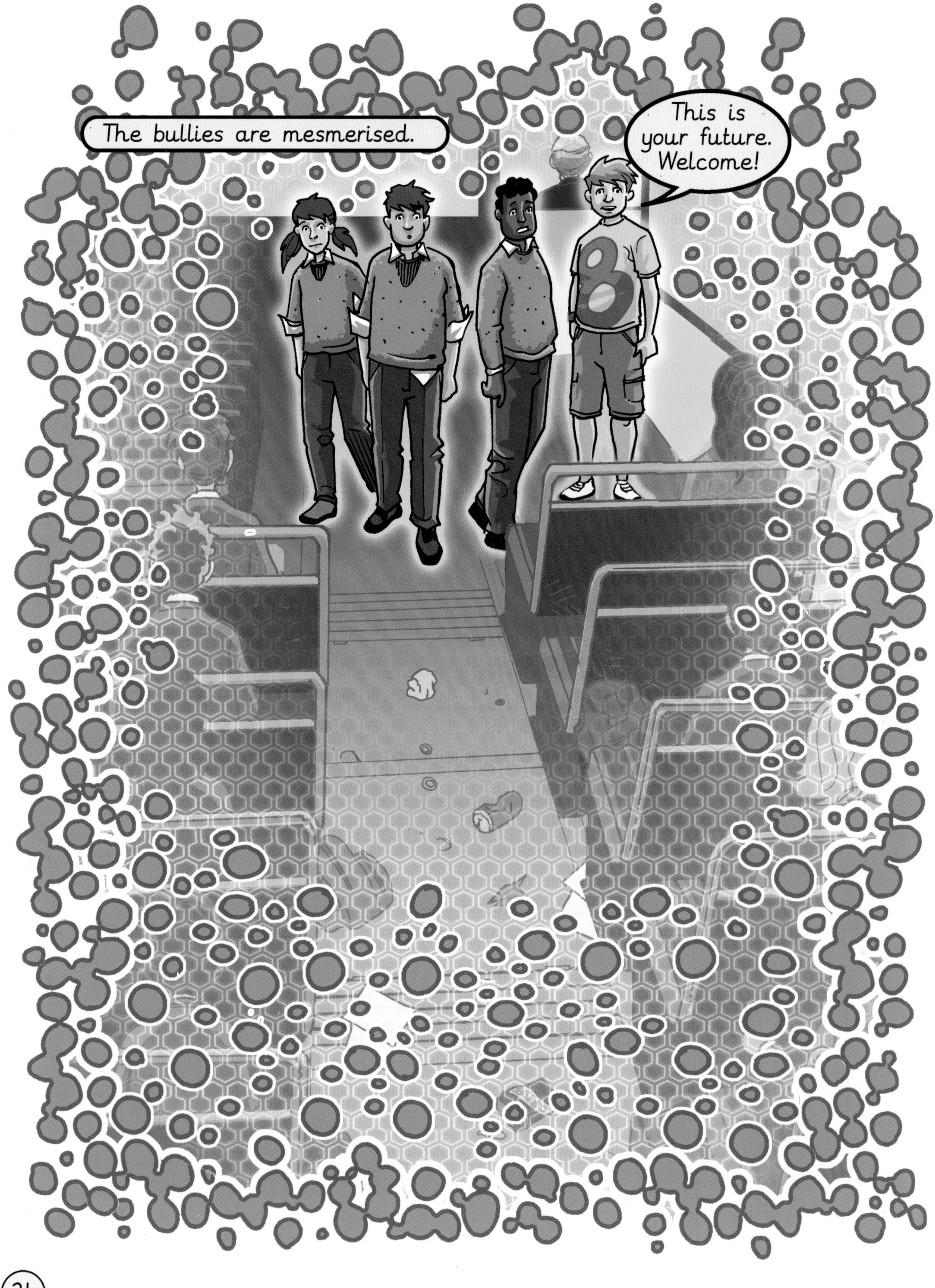
The bullies are mesmerised.
This is your future. Welcome!

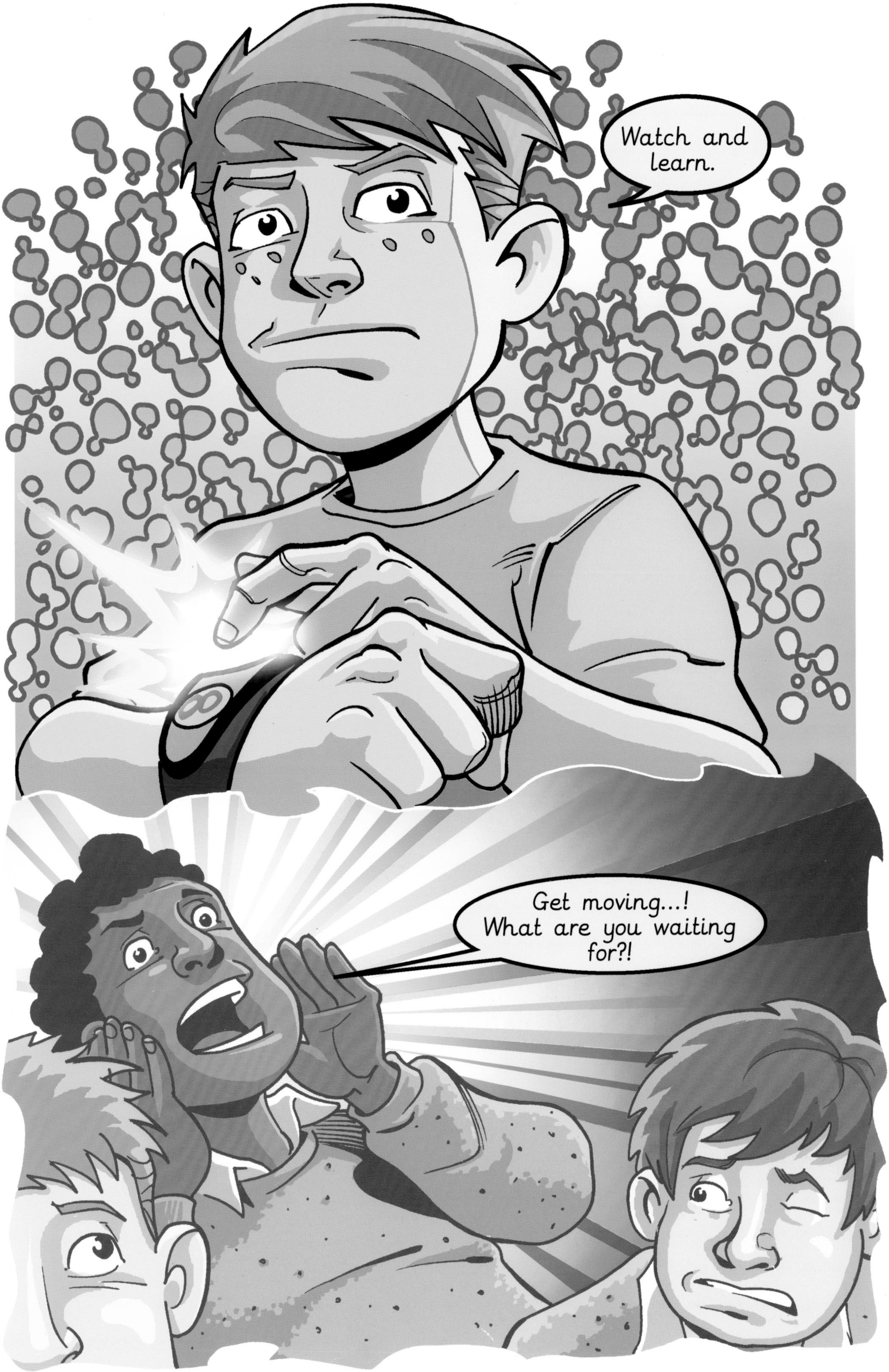
Watch and learn.
Get moving...! What are you waiting for?!

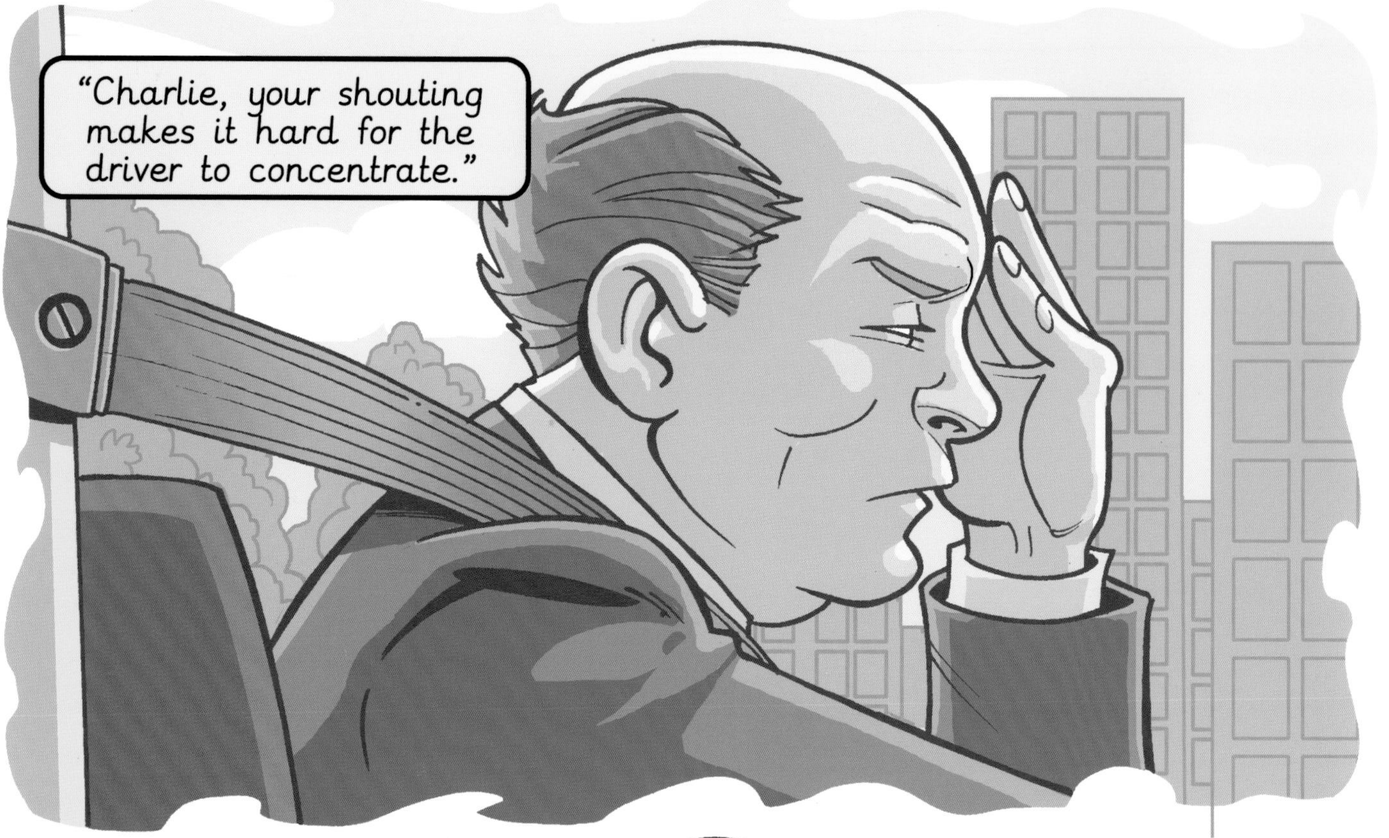
"Charlie, your shouting makes it hard for the driver to concentrate."

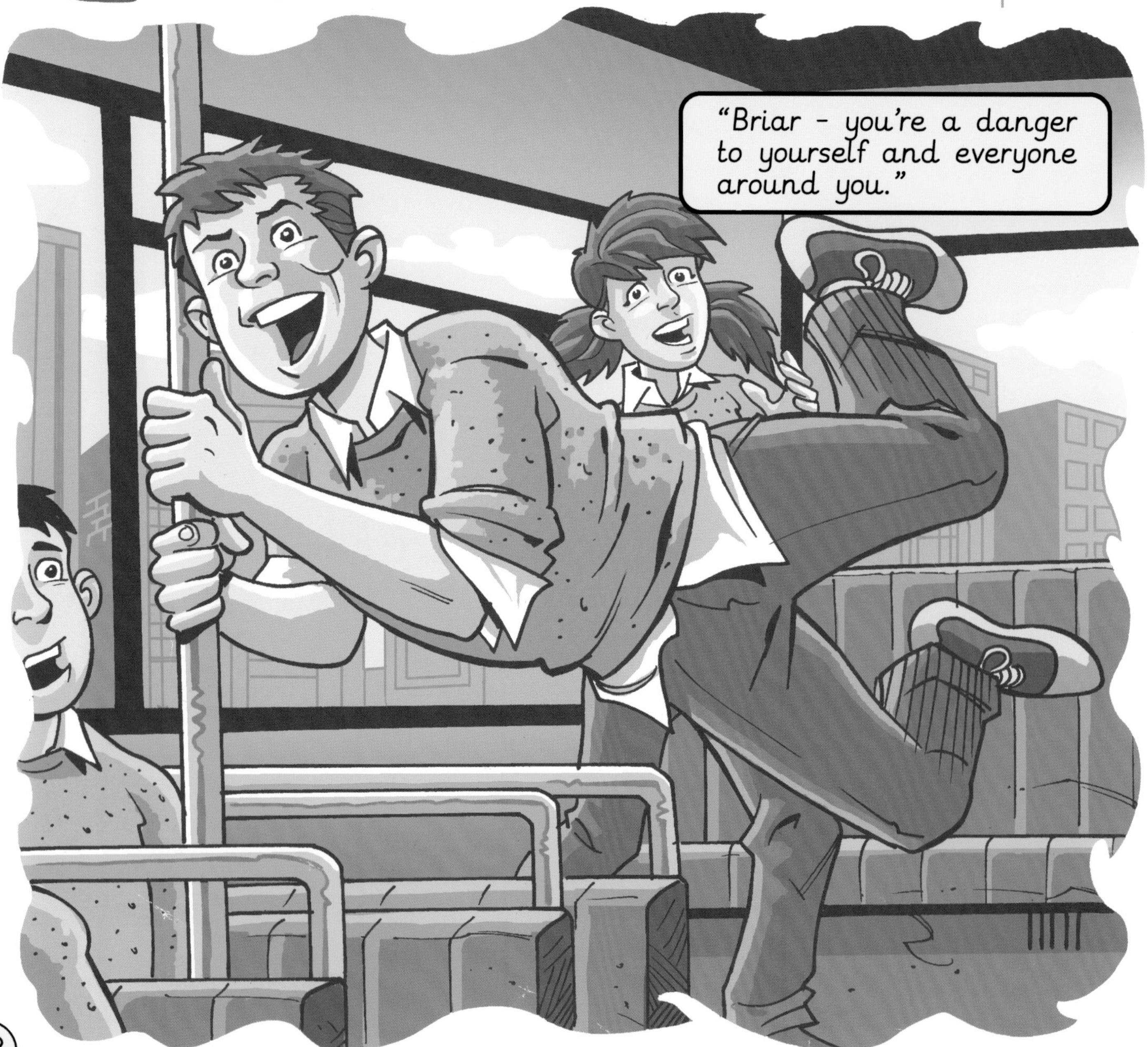
"Briar - you're a danger to yourself and everyone around you."

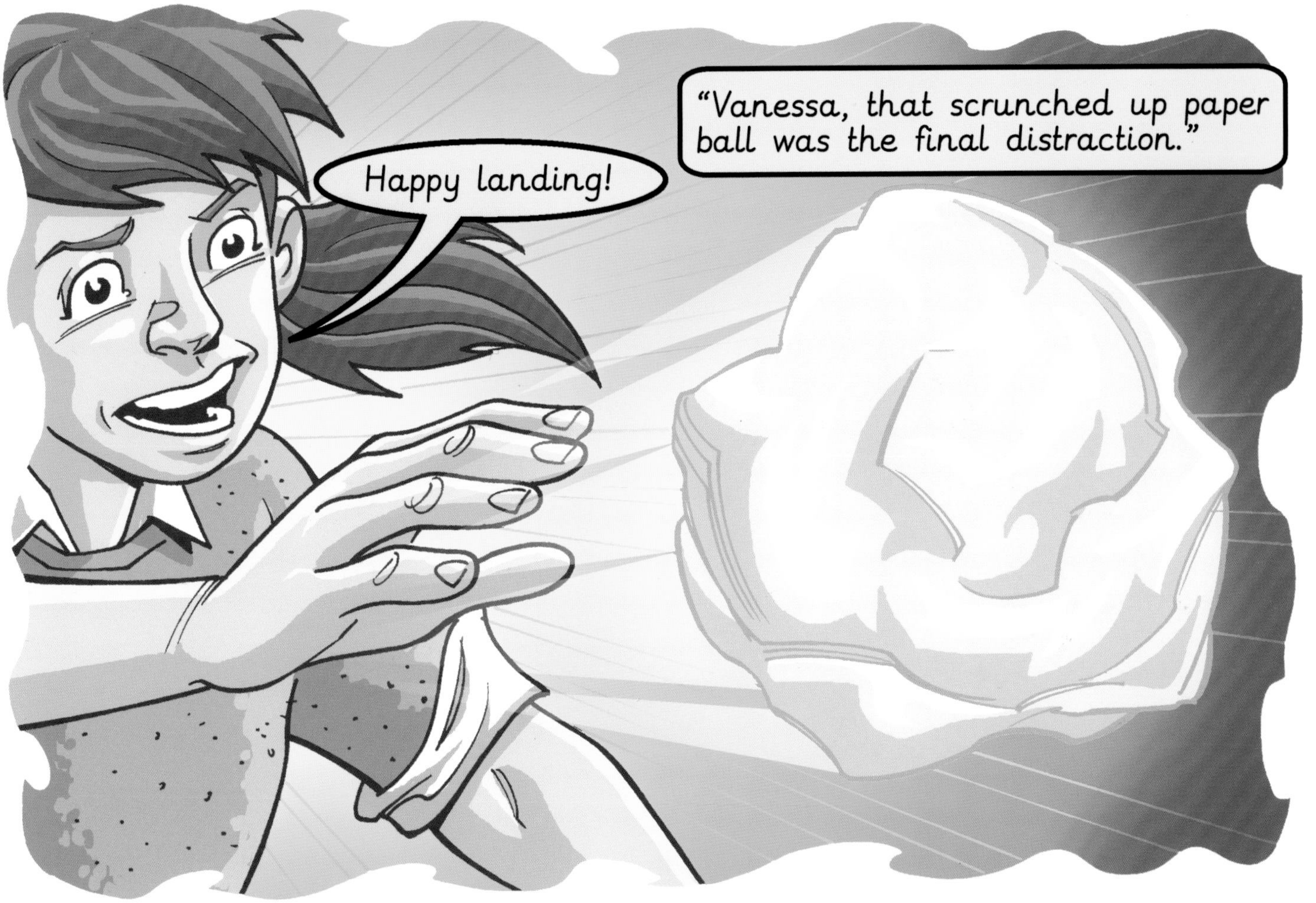
Happy landing!
"Vanessa, that scrunched up paper ball was the final distraction."

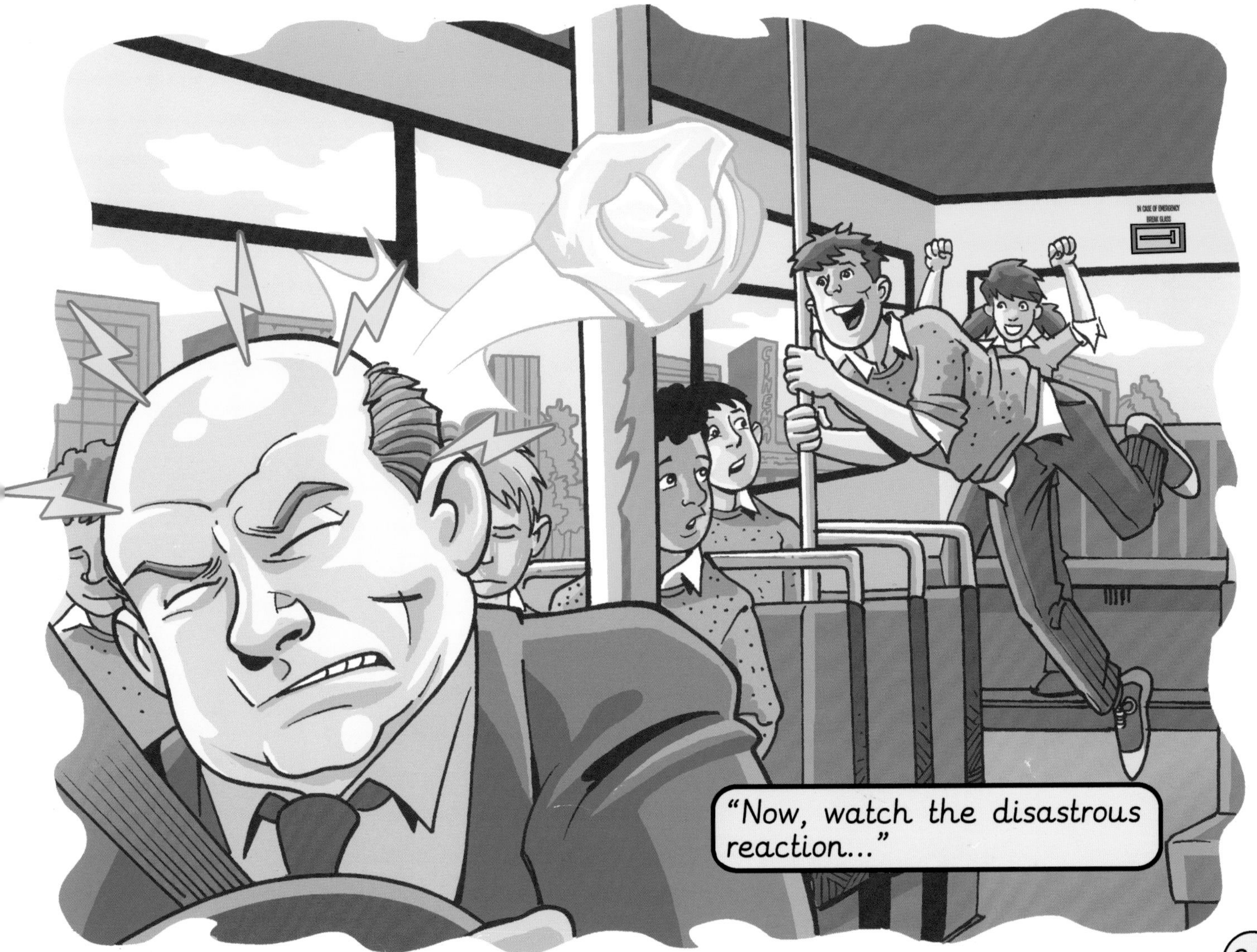
"Now, watch the disastrous reaction..."

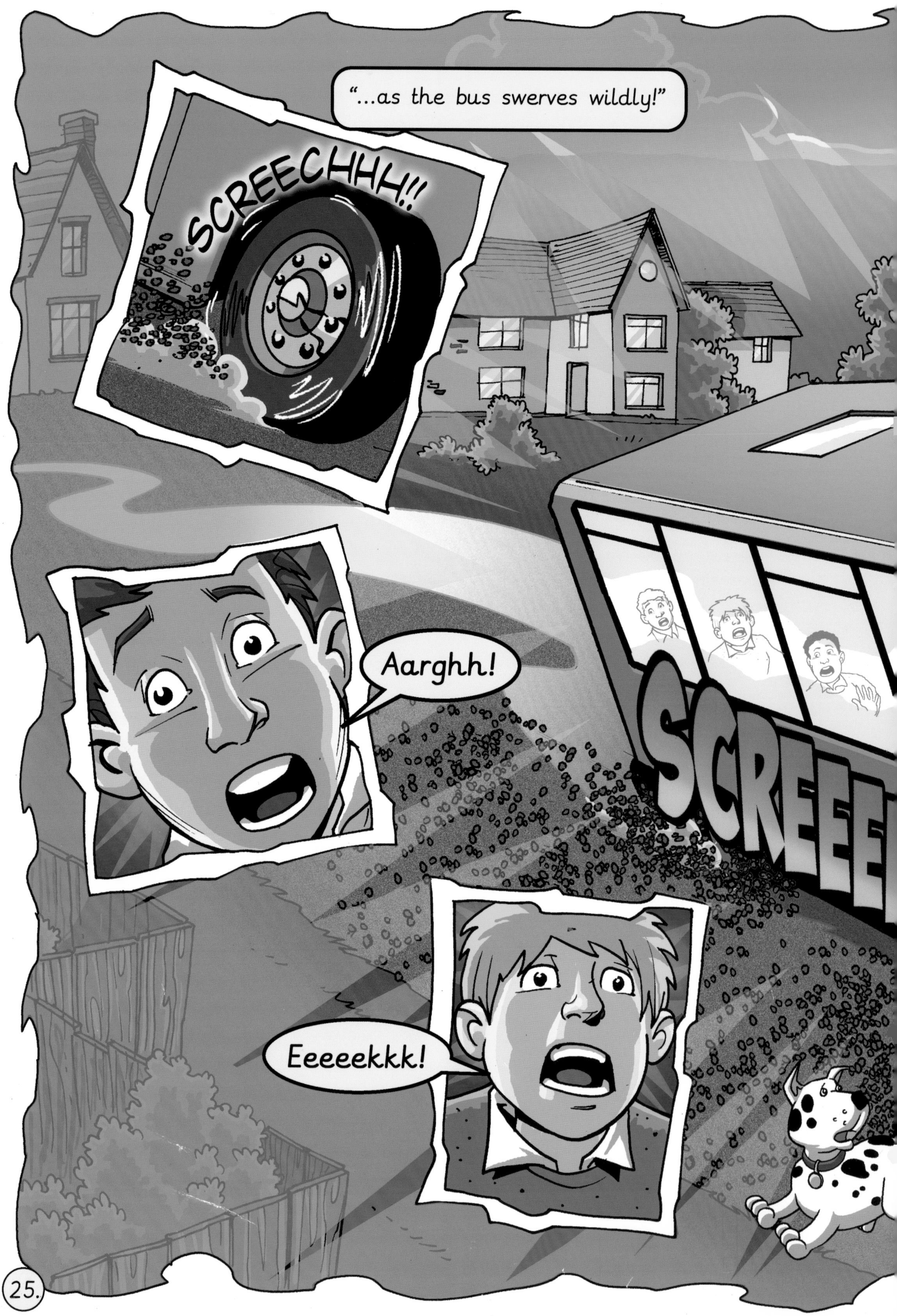
"...as the bus swerves wildly!"
SCREECHHH!!
Aarghh!
SCREEE
Eeeeekkk!

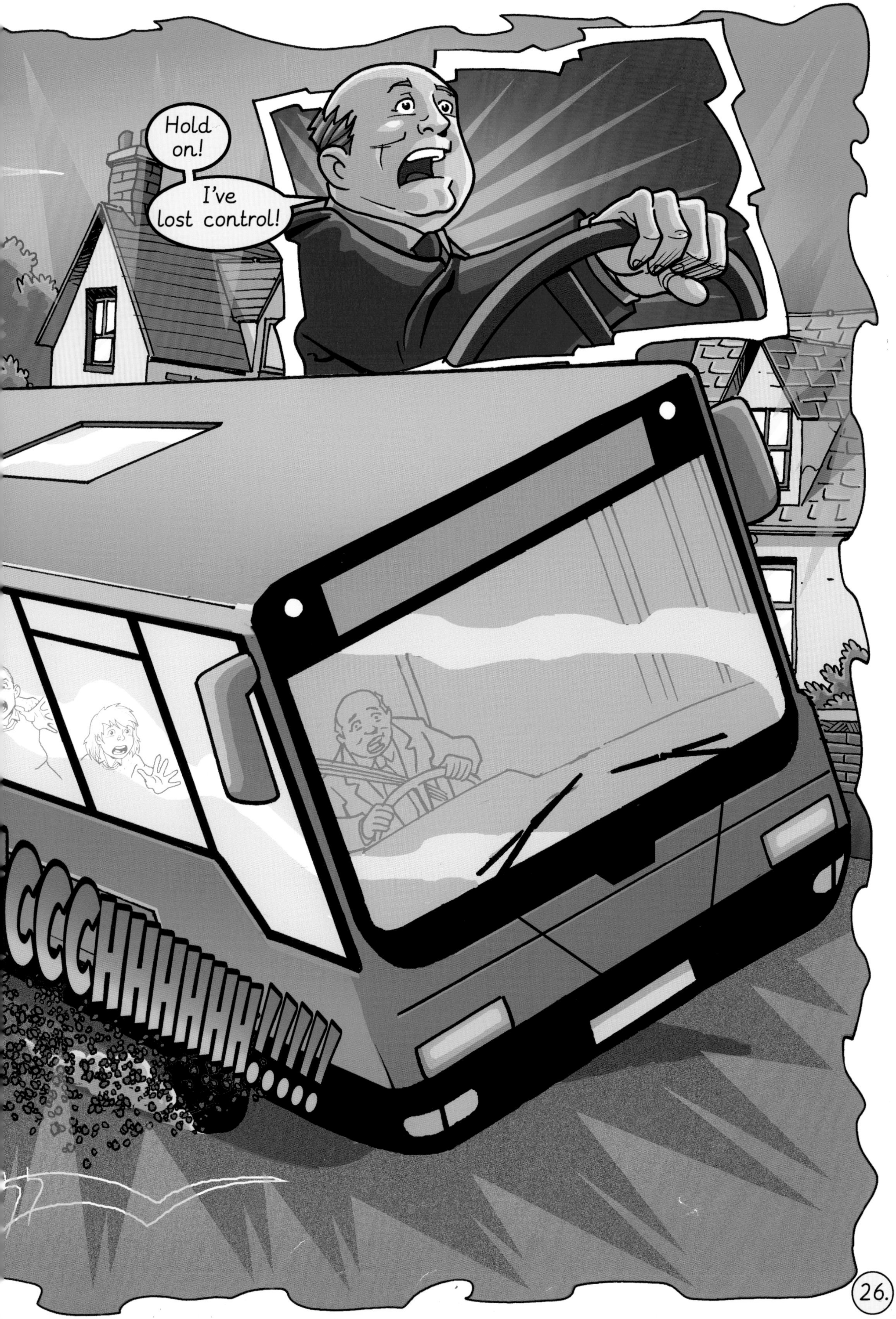
Hold on!
I've lost control!
CCCHHHHHH!!!!!.....

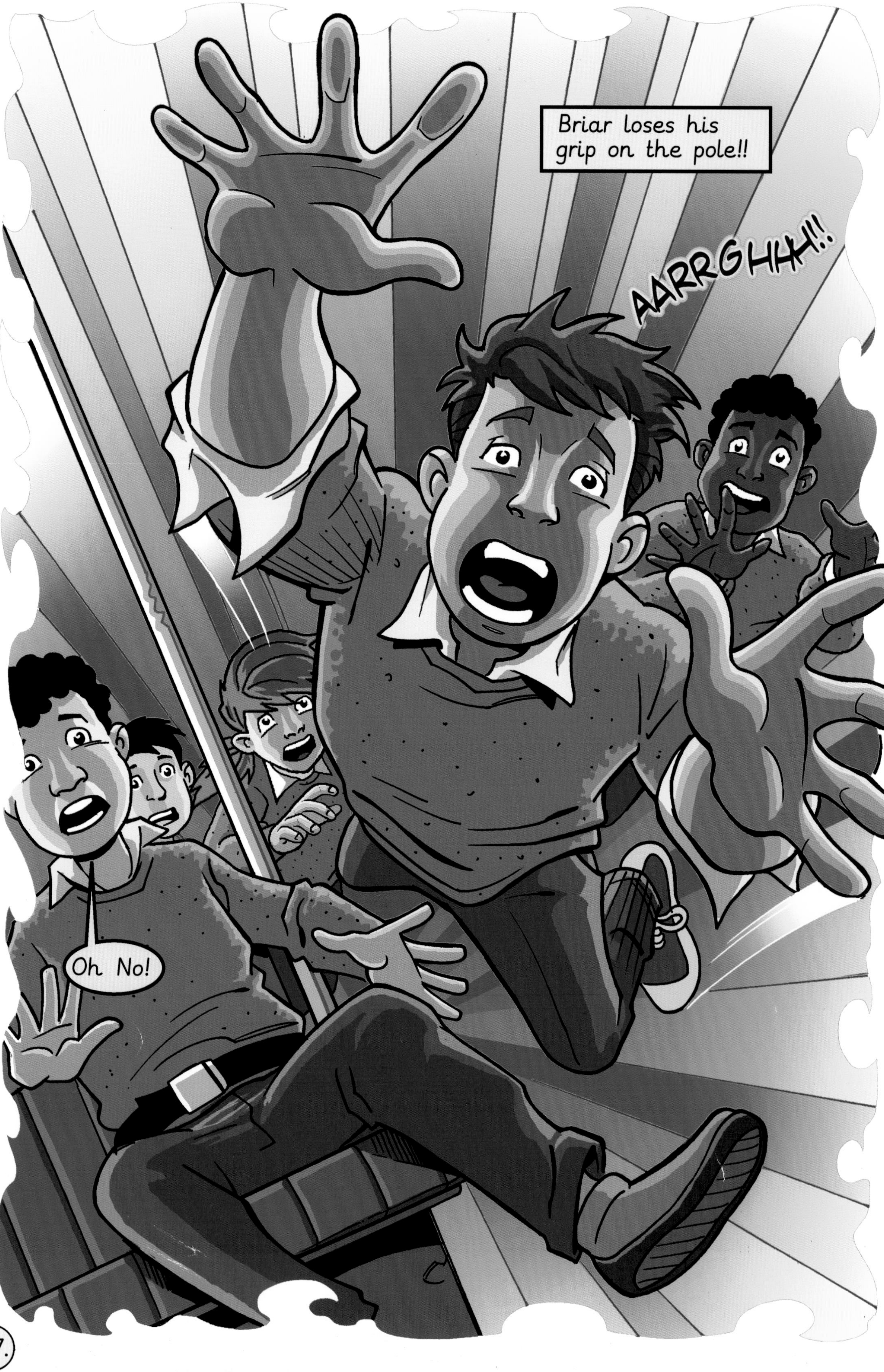
Briar loses his grip on the pole!!
AARRGHHH!!
Oh No!

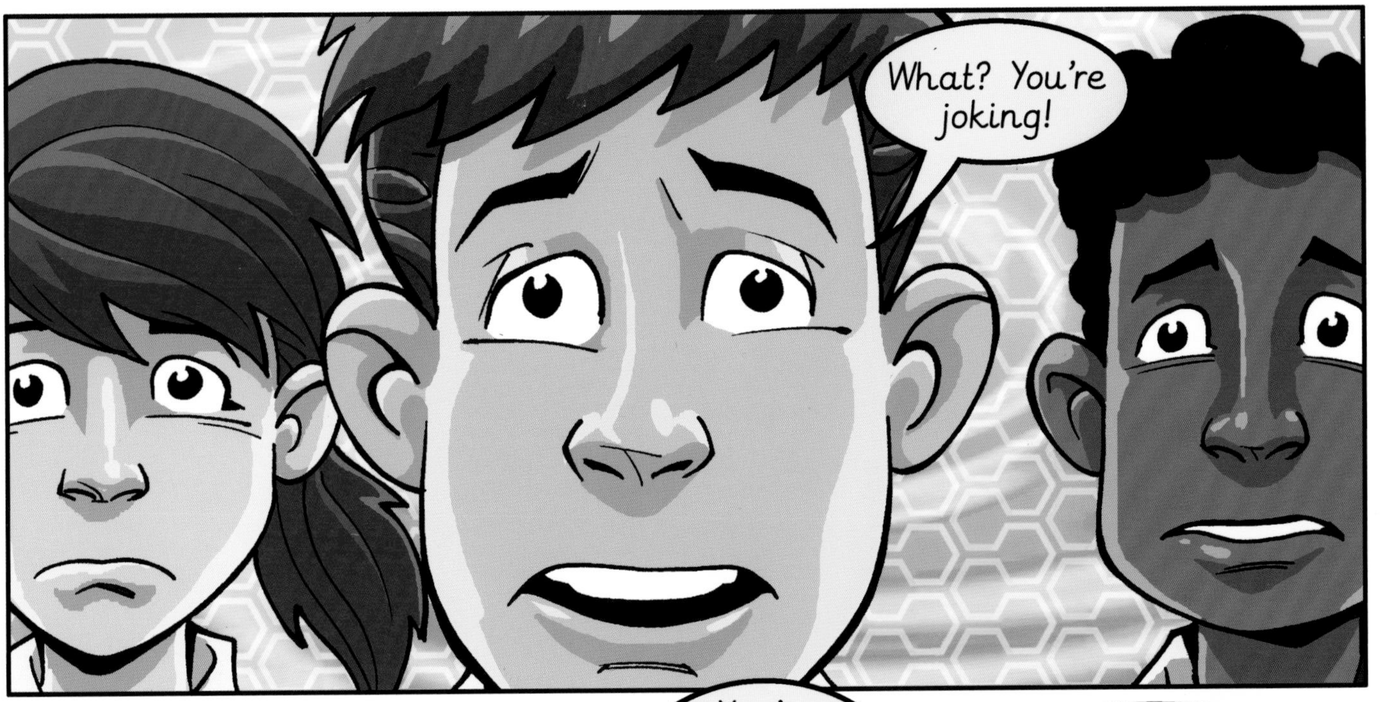
What? You're joking!

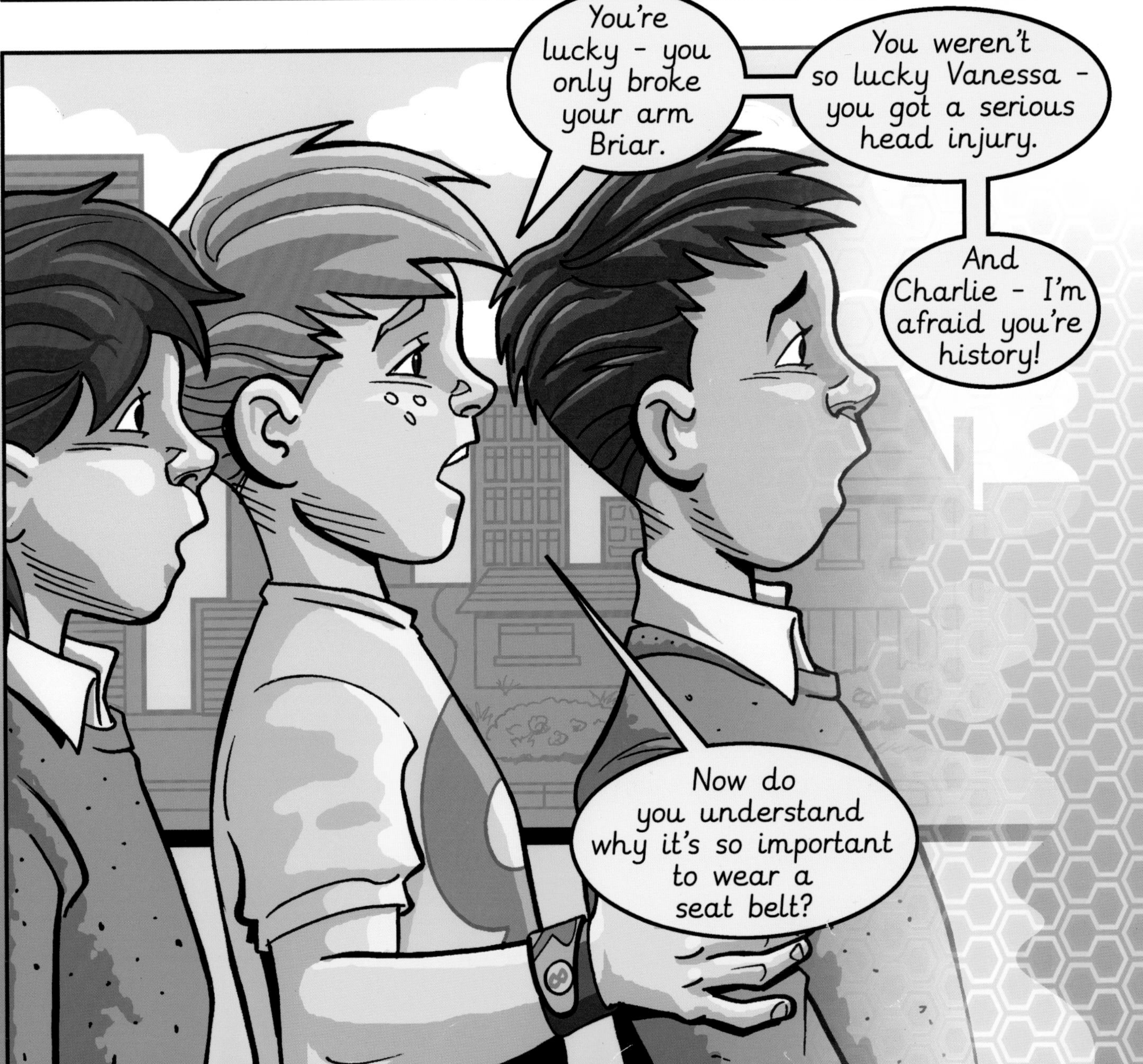
You're lucky - you only broke your arm Briar.
You weren't so lucky Vanessa - you got a serious head injury.
And Charlie - I'm afraid you're history!
Now do you understand why it's so important to wear a seat belt?

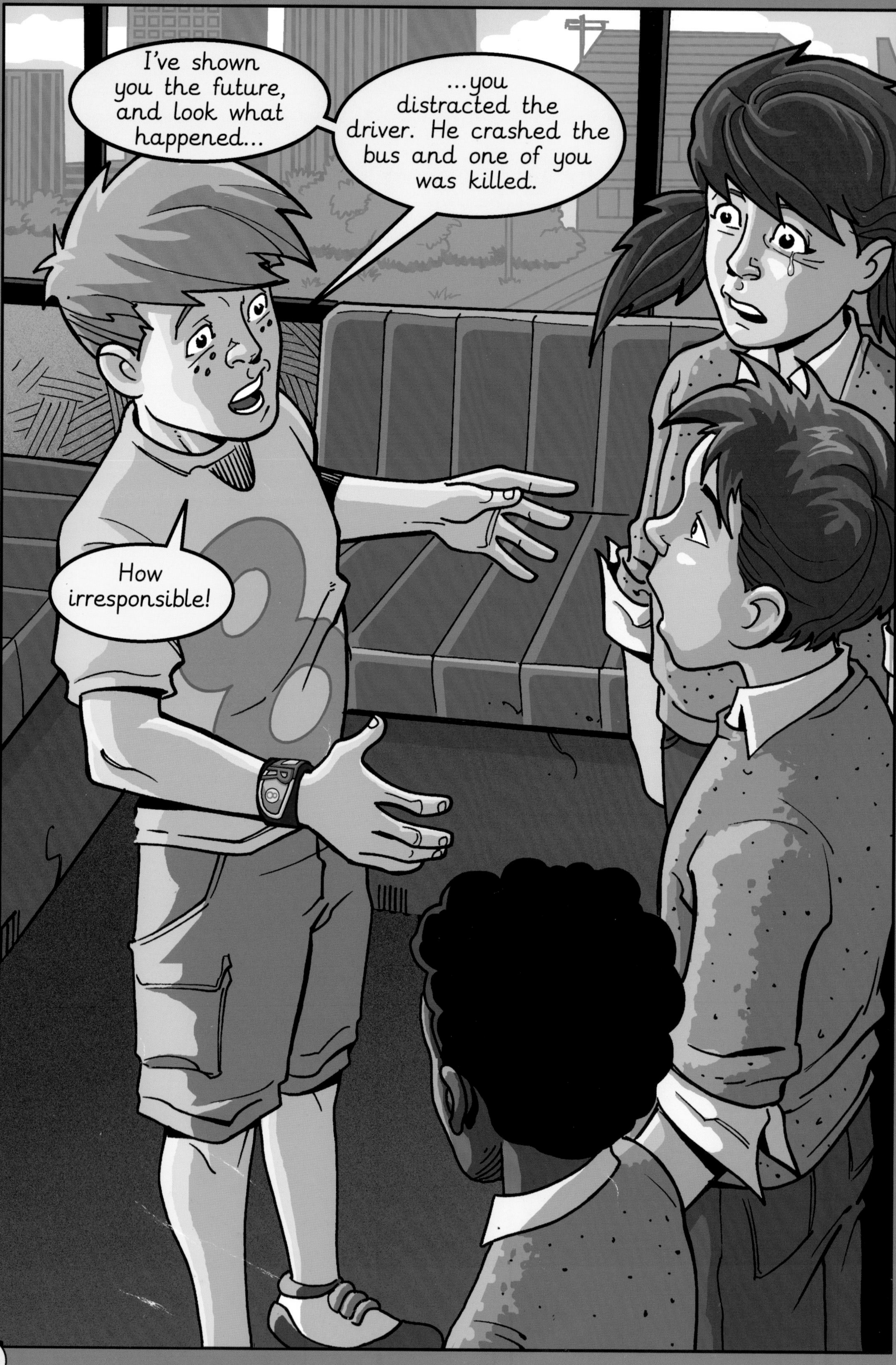

I've shown you the future, and look what happened...
...you distracted the driver. He crashed the bus and one of you was killed.
How irresponsible!

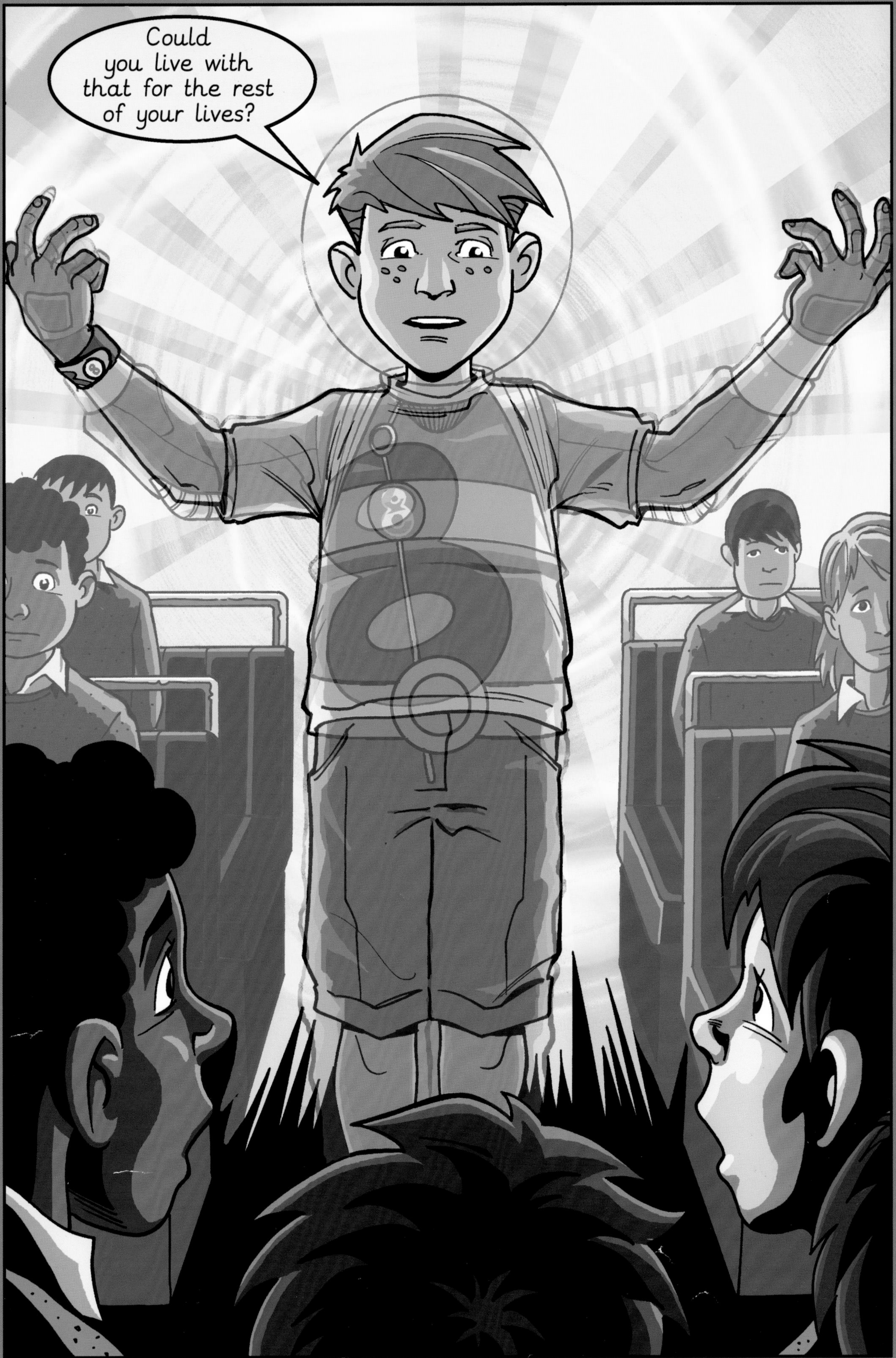
Could you live with that for the rest of your lives?

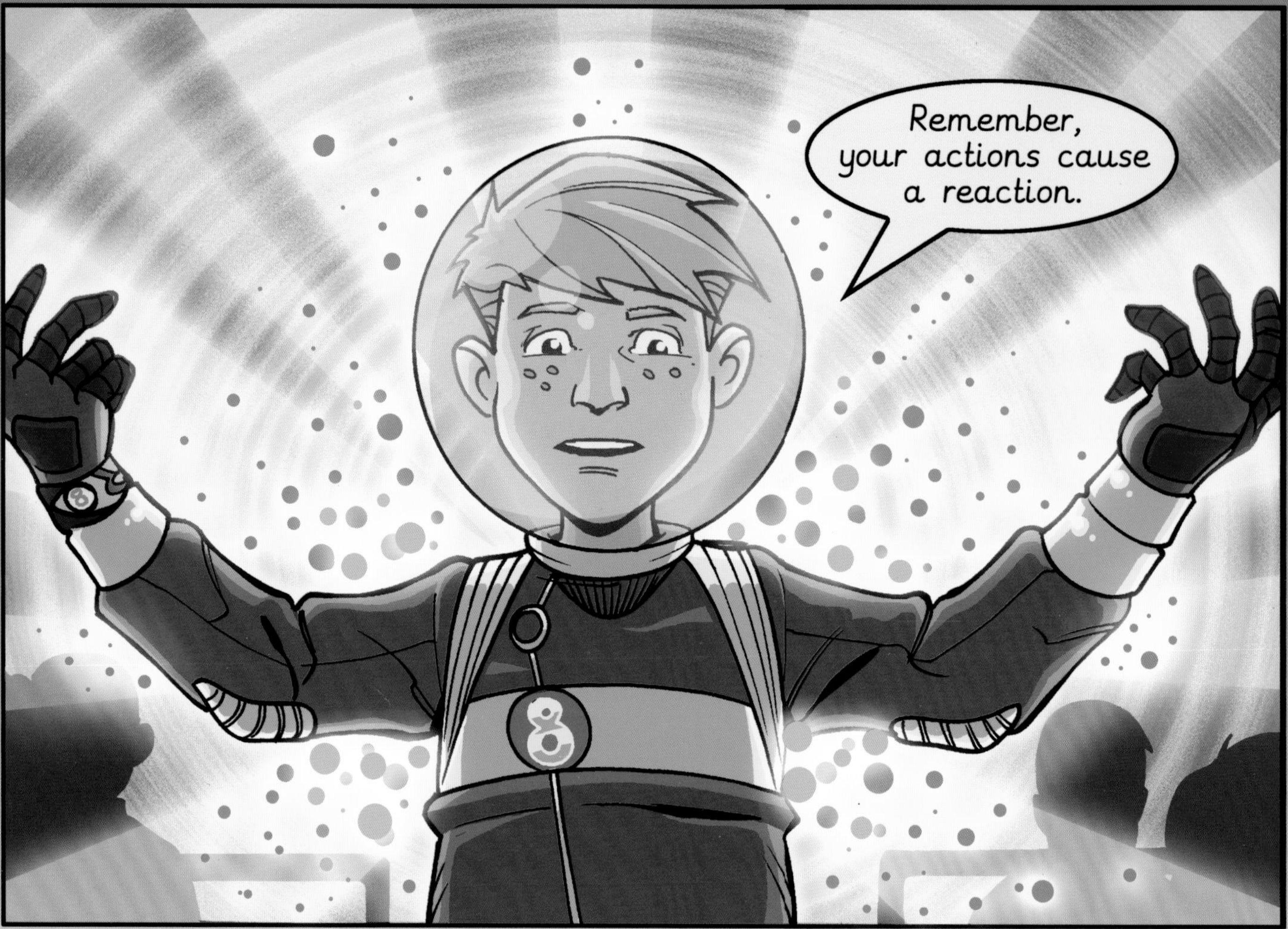
Remember, your actions cause a reaction.

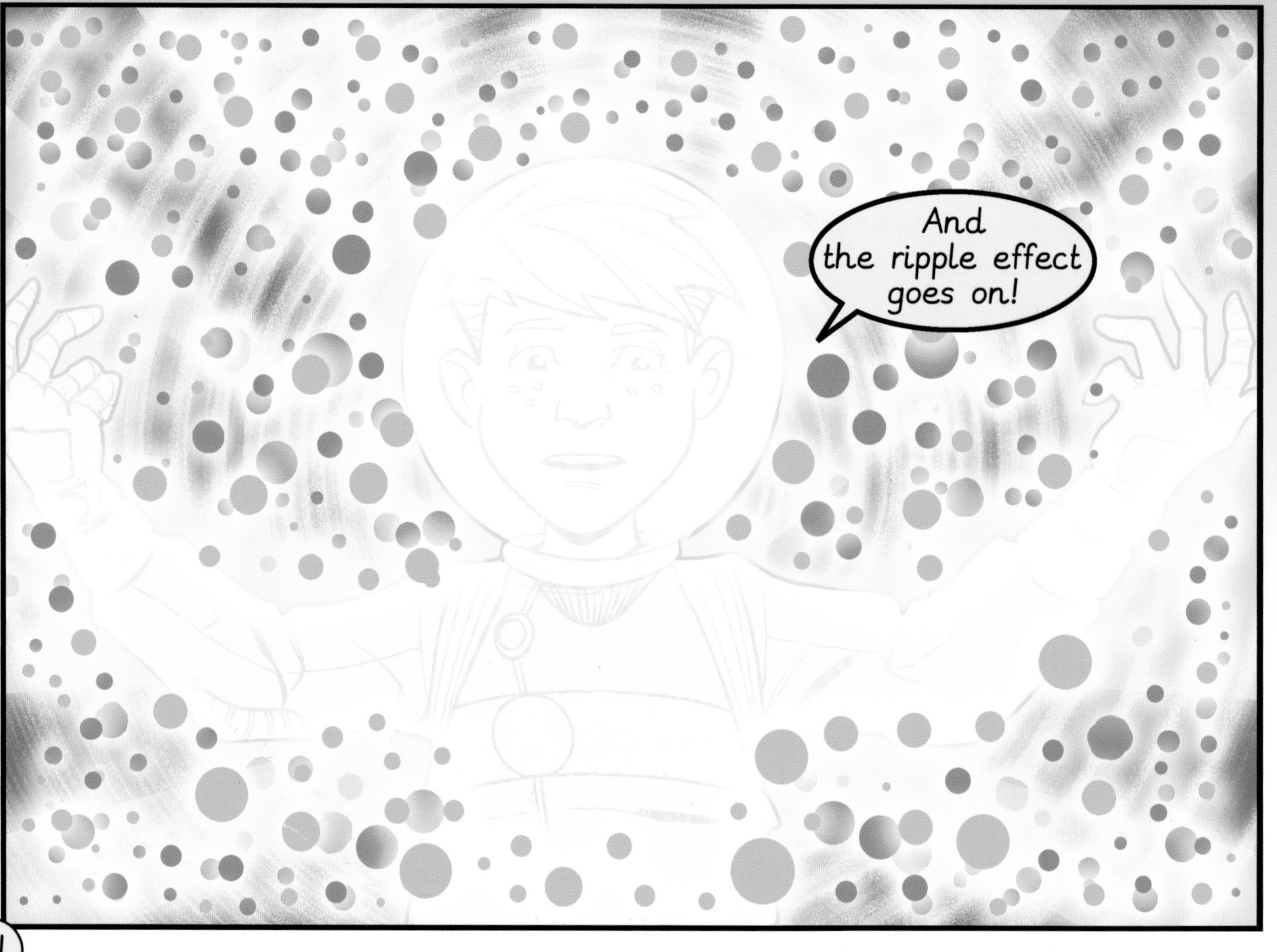
And the ripple effect goes on!

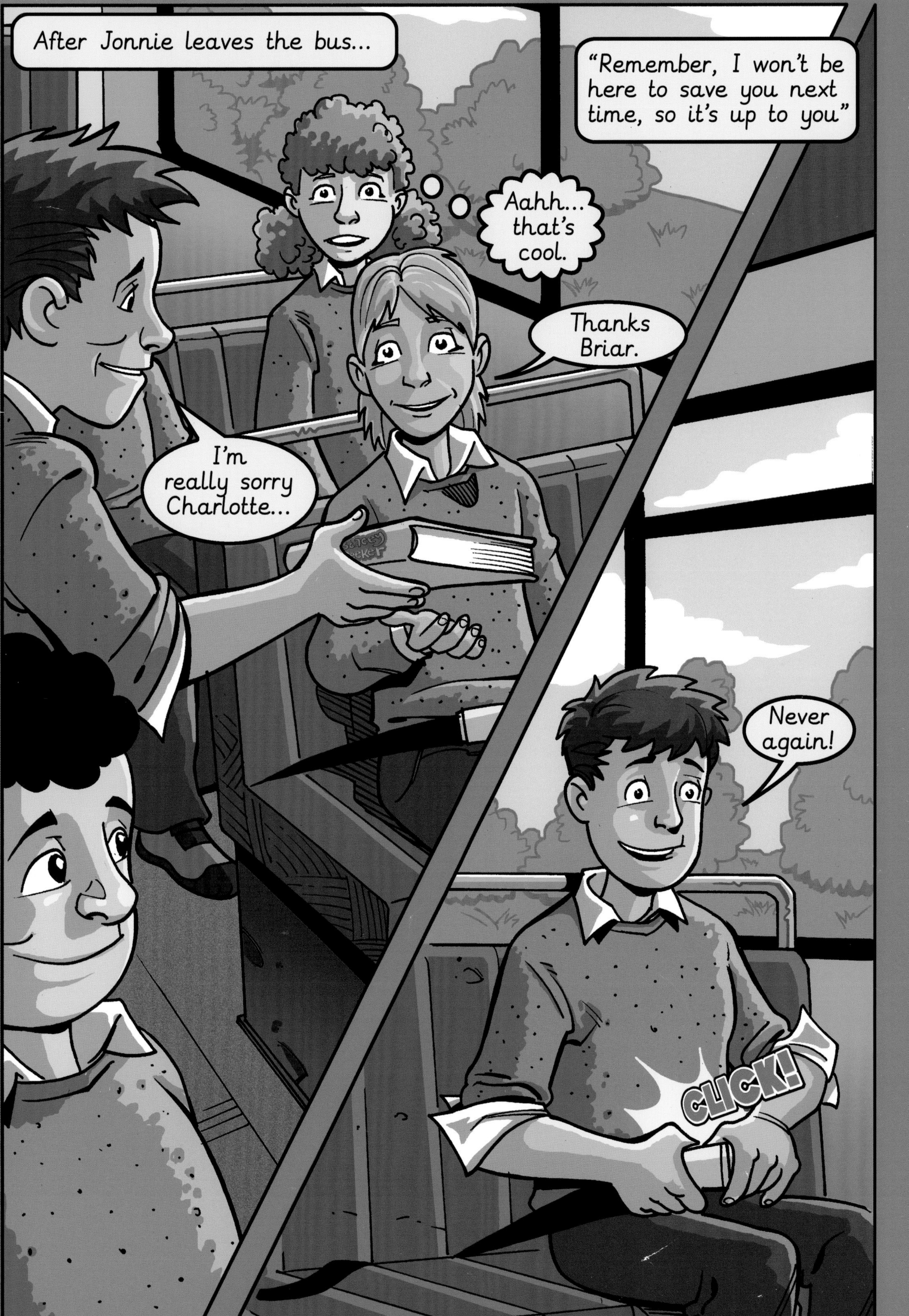
After Jonnie leaves the bus...
"Remember, I won't be here to save you next time, so it's up to you"
Aahh... that's cool.
Thanks Briar.
I'm really sorry Charlotte...
Never again!
CLICK!

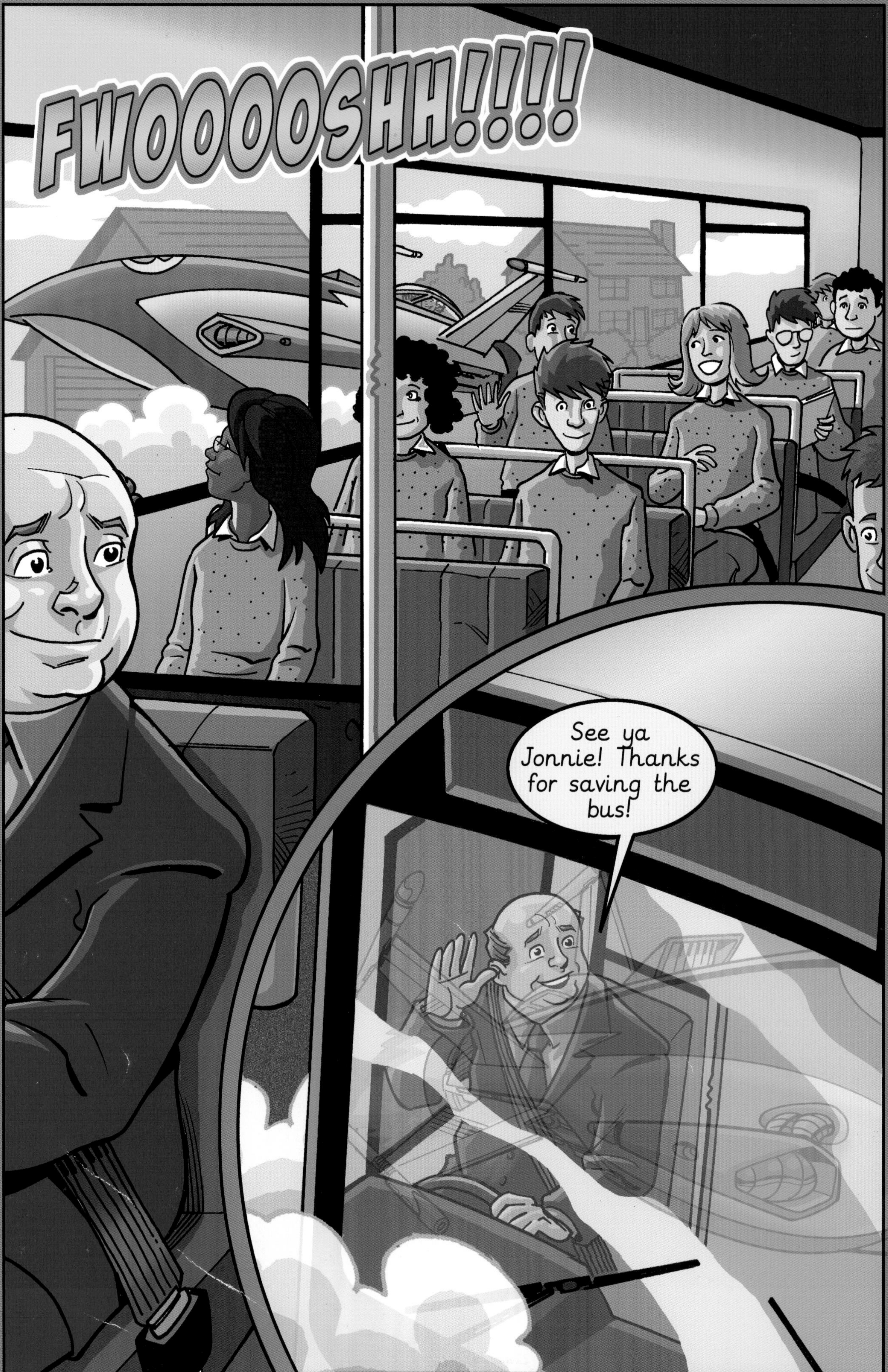
FWOOOOSHH!!!!
See ya Jonnie! Thanks for saving the bus!

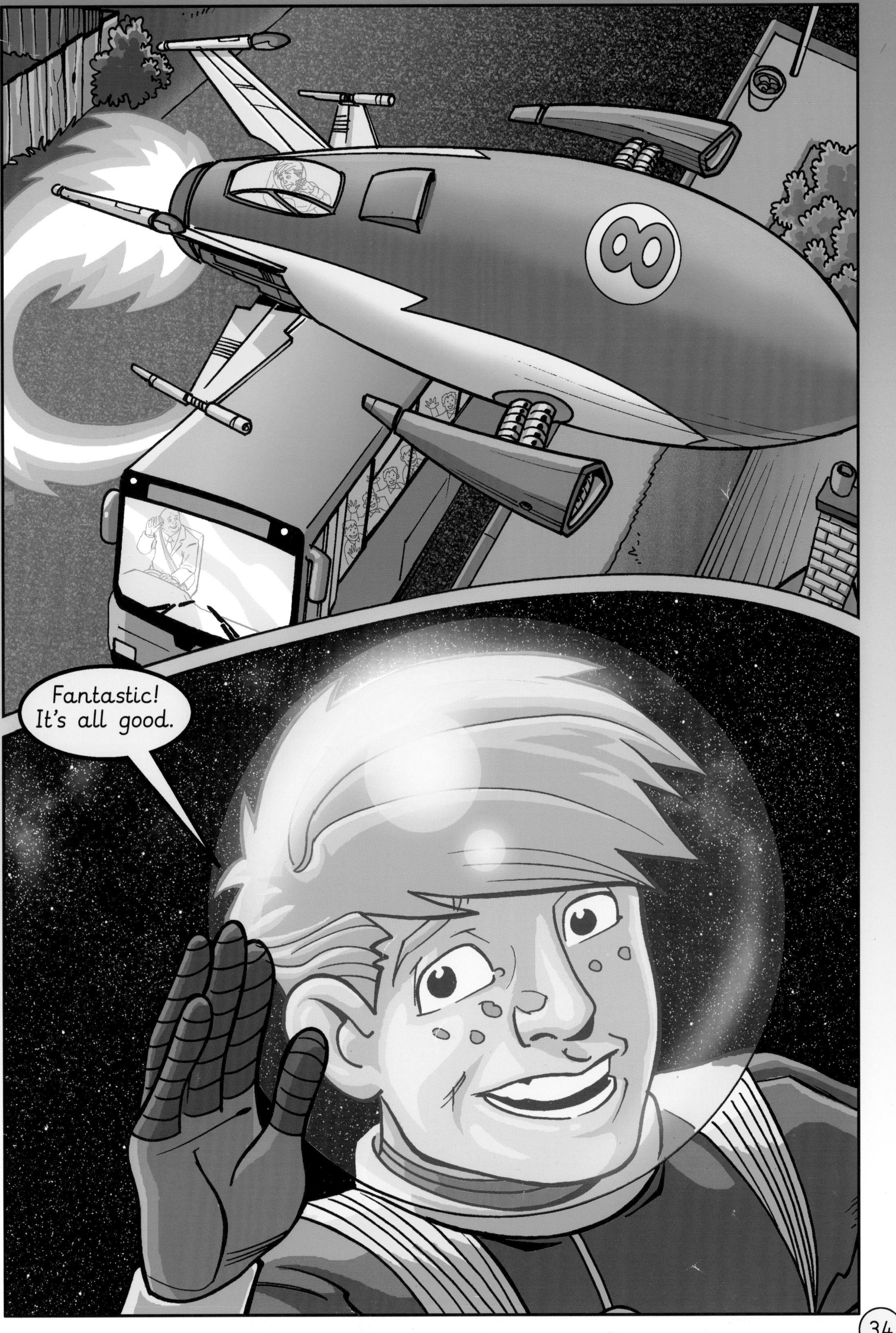
8
Fantastic!
It's all good.

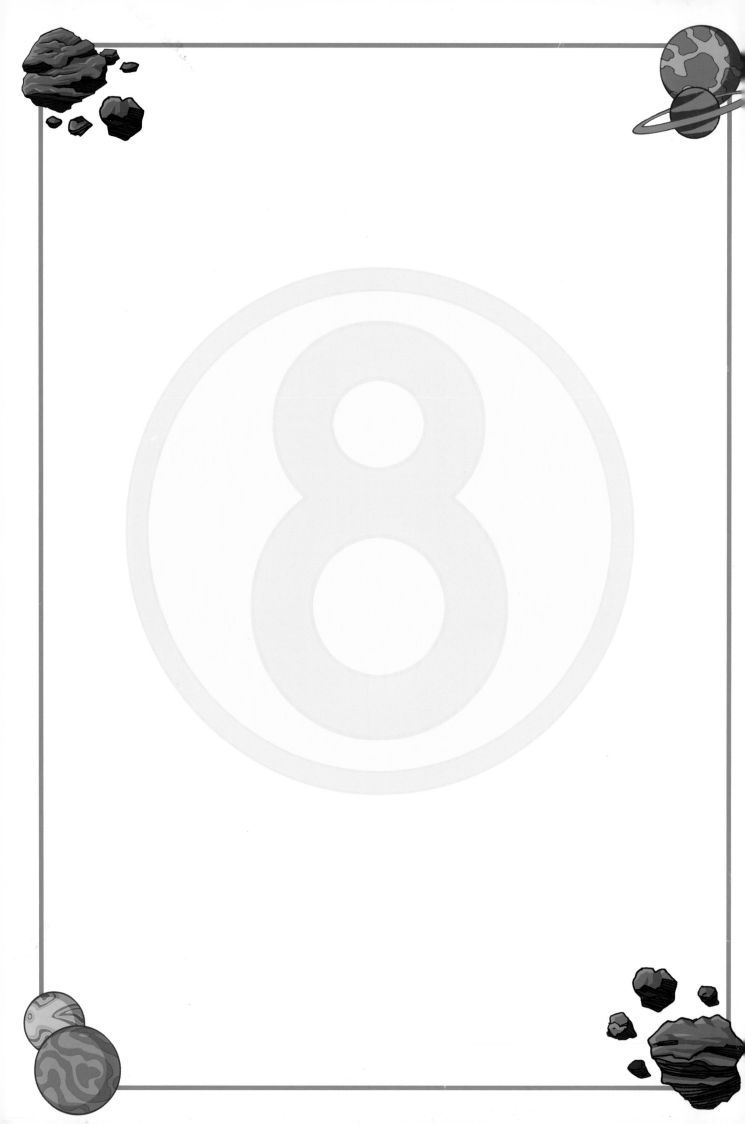

About the Author
John Chapman - Creator, Author

As a young boy, the wonder of the universe and a love of cycling had always been close to John's heart. Growing up in the 1960s John had begun to form the first concepts of an idea through his strong imagination and creative role-playing. He dreamt of rocket-ships and space adventures, and was passionate about his bicycle and the escapism it gave him. Therefore it was no surprise that in 1998 John had the idea for his imaginary character Jonnie Rocket.

With the creation of this character firmly embedded in John's imagination he spent the next two years formulating the idea; compiling the draft of his first book 'The Adventures of Jonnie Rocket' in the year 2000. He wrote this initial book as a scripted storyboard, with the aim of animating the character of Jonnie Rocket as a TV series.

John has since created a collection of stories, centred on 'The Adventures of Jonnie Rocket', twelve of which will be published in book form.

As part of John's imaginary space adventure, it was with some irony that in 1976 he found himself making a brief appearance as an X-Wing pilot in 'Star Wars (A New Hope)', living out the dream of a space adventurer through the most iconic sci-fi film of all time! Bringing Jonnie Rocket to life after four decades must surely be John Chapman's intention....

The Adventures of Jonnie Rocket: Books in the Series

THE ADVENTURES OF
JONNIE ROCKET
JOHN CHAPMAN

THE ADVENTURES OF JONNIE ROCKET

ISBN: 978-0-9573035-0-8

Jonnie, aged 8, battles with Space Pirates and visits Zuke, a very strange planet.

THE ADVENTURES OF
JONNIE ROCKET
SAGA 1
JOHN CHAPMAN

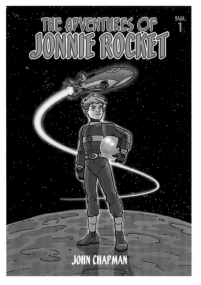

SAGA 1: THE RIDE OF TERROR

ISBN: 978-0-9573035-2-2

Jonnie, now aged 12, is on a mission to save the school bus. Will he succeed, or have the bullies gone too far this time?

THE ADVENTURES OF
JONNIE ROCKET
SAGA 2
JOHN CHAPMAN

SAGA 2: THE SPACE LOBES

ISBN: 978-0-9573035-1-5

Jonnie crashes on Planet Cranium and meets the alien Space Lobes.

THE ADVENTURES OF
JONNIE ROCKET
SAGA 3
JOHN CHAPMAN

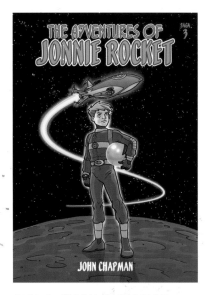

SAGA 3: THE SEA OF SARGOSS

ISBN: 978-0-9573035-3-9

Dr Avatar sends Jonnie to Sargoss, which is facing an ecological disaster of devastating proportions. Can he save the universe?

Become a Rocketeer: visit www.jonnierocket.com and learn more about Jonnie's world!